THE GUARDIAN
OF ISIS

Monica Hughes

HOUGHTON MIFFLIN COMPANY BOSTON

Atlanta   Dallas   Geneva, Illinois   Palo Alto   Princeton   Toronto

Introduction

A stellar cruiser, blinking into real space five parsecs from Earth, in the neighbourhood of the constellation Indus, picked up a message beamed from the fourth planet of the F-type star Ra. The message confirmed the cruiser's space co-ordinates, and continued with a warning to the ship to keep its distance and under no circumstances to approach or land on the fourth planet of the star system. Quarantine conditions in effect, the message went on: original Earth population in Primitive Agricultural Phase, not to be disturbed.

It was the Earth-year 2136 A.D. The message had been beamed out into the lonely reaches of space since soon after the settlement's first beginnings. It would be beamed, if the Guardian deemed necessary, for a thousand years more...

Chapter One

"JODY!"

The voice echoed from the great cliff wall of the mesa and bounced around his ears like fifty irritating aunties calling him. Jody hunched his shoulders and went on with what he was doing.

At the head of the lake, where the river entered, still foaming from its furious descent from the high country, the water shot over small rocks and ledges in a miniature version of the Cascades, the triple waterfall that blocked the north end of the Valley. All through the winter Jody had thought about the river, falling from the heights and pounding the basin at the foot of the Cascades with such force that the rocks trembled and the air was filled with spray and thunder. So much *power*, all going to waste.

"JODY!"

—If you could make the water *do* something as it fell from the high country into the Valley, something like turning a wheel, then you could do . . . do what? What use was a wheel turning and turning by itself, way up at the head of the Valley? Jody felt as if he was on the edge of a tremendous discovery. It hovered inside his head, tantalisingly just out of reach.

He squatted at the water's edge, his eyes on the bamboo model he had lashed together, watching the water fill the miniature troughs he had painstakingly made from split stems. The wheel spun. The troughs filled, fell, and emptied . . . If he had a long shaft instead of just an axle, then the shaft would spin too. He could feel the idea coming closer. It was like one of the big white cactus moths that were so hard to catch. They fluttered from cactus bloom to bloom, until you could just about put your hand on their fragile wings. And then . . .

"Jody N'Kumo!" The voice was almost in his ears, and he rocked forward and nearly fell into the water. The thought that had been just within his grasp fluttered off into the dark insides of his mind.

"Oh, bother it! Auntie, why did you have to do that?"

1

"Why didn't you answer me then? I called enough times. Till I'm hoarse. What are you up to anyway?" She peered over his shoulder and clicked her tongue against her teeth. "Toys! And you a Third. I don't understand you, boy. Here we are only one day away from Thanksgiving and all of us working from Ra-up to Ra-down, and you're playing with toys!"

"It's not a . . ."

"It wouldn't be so bad if you were only a Fourth, but you're not. You're a Third and that means responsibility. All the Fourths look up to you." Auntie had started out moderately enough, but now she began to scold herself into a passion. "It's too bad. Really it is. Even the smallest ones are busy husking winter-berries for the pies, and here is Jody N'Kumo, grandson of the sister of the President, mooning with his toys by the river!"

"It wasn't like that," Jody muttered.

"And don't stick your lip out that way, or you'll trip over it," she snapped. Hands on hips, apron blowing in the wind, she stood over him as he scrambled to his feet. The stream shot over the smooth slab of rock and hit the blades of the tiny water-wheel, so that it spun faster and faster. He bent to pick it up.

"You just leave that be. It won't run away. You can come back and play later, *after* the work is all done, if you please. Here's your lunch." She handed him a large woven grass bag and a packet wrapped in pandus leaves. "All the Fourths with legs long enough for it are walking across the Valley already. You'll have to hurry to catch them up. Be sure to check every trap and snare, or it'll be a thin Thanksgiving we'll have this year. Have you got your sling?" She barely gave him time to feel for the loop of smooth leather at his belt before she was off again. "Bring home a couple of plump purple-furs or a rock-bunny, and maybe I'll forget to report to the Council that you've wasted the better part of the morning playing."

"I wasn't . . . Oh, all right, Auntie. I'm off." He jumped from stone to stone over the flashing river and began to run across the short wiry blue-grass that covered the stony slopes below the mesa.

Jody seethed inside as he ran, the empty game bag bumping at his belt, the lunch packet hitched to the other side for balance. Nobody took him seriously. Nobody was a real friend. To the

2

elders and the Council he was the troublesome N'Kumo boy who was always asking questions instead of doing his allotted tasks. To his father he was a shame, to his mother a constant source of worry. She was the one who suffered the most from the waspish tongues of the aunties, those old biddies with nothing better to do than to spy on other people's children and make mischief. It wasn't fair...

Even among the younger people in the Valley Jody saw himself gloomily as of no account. His Grandfather was the youngest of the Firsts, and since Jody was the youngest child in his family, almost an afterthought, he was far and away the youngest of the Thirds. He was the only one among them not married, and therefore not entitled to attend Council meetings, nor to vote or have his opinions listened to by anybody.

The Fourths, fifteen of whom were in fact the same age as Jody, kept their distance and were never really that friendly. After all, he was a *Third*, the same generation as their parents and aunts and uncles! Yet he was for ever condemned to do the same chores and perform the same rites as them, just because he was too young to be a man.

Jody sighed and looked across the wide, grass-filled Valley. Taller than head-high, the grass hid the Fourths from him, but he could see the red plumes shake and nod as the boys searched this way and that for forgotten traps and snares. Only the boys. The girls would be stuck at home, with the delightful chore of plucking and drawing the birds already collected for the feast, and scrubbing and preparing the vegetables.

The thought of the girls cheered him up a little. He might be the lowest form of life on Isis, but at least he hadn't been born a girl. With a sudden insight he glimpsed the life that made the aunties bitter and waspish, that made his mother look occasionally at Father as if he were an enemy. Why were women inferior? The never-before-asked question came to him so suddenly that he broke stride and stumbled on a tussock of grass.

If the legends *were* true, unlikely though it seemed, and the people of Isis *had* come through the sky from a star called Earth, then it must have been both men and women who came. Surely the journey would have been as difficult—as unimaginably difficult—for men and women alike? So why were women now of such little account on Isis? What had gone wrong?

3

It was just one more of the many questions to which Jody had no answer. One more question that he knew by now not to ask. He recovered from his stumble and jogged doggedly on towards the western end of the Valley. Let the Fourths beat through the grass-land after forgotten traps and snares. It was in his mind to keep to the short grass at the Valley's rim, where running was easy, and reach the far end, where the tall red-grass ended, before them.

It had been a bad spring. There had been only grudging rains the previous summer and the grazing was consequently poor. During the short days of winter the hunters had watched their precious game scramble up out of the Valley into the mountain passes, braving the cold and the unbreathably thin air, to seek unknown valleys beyond, where the grazing might be better— valleys that were taboo, where the hunters might not follow them.

Jody thought it was stupid to hold Thanksgiving in the spring, when there was nothing to eat but scrawny meat and the end of the winter's supply of dried fruit and nuts, withered vegetables and grain. By midsummer there would be feasts worthy of the name. Fat fish and fowl. Juicy swelling summer- berries. Even the occasional comb of wild honey. His mouth watered at the thought and his stomach gave a sudden twinge.

He hunkered down on a smooth rock, warm with Ra's heat, and spread out his lunch on the pandus leaves. Not much for a growing boy, almost a man. Everything must be going into the larders for tomorrow's feast. A hunk of bread, none too fresh. A wedge of cheese, bloomy with mould at its outer edge. A handful of wizened winter-berries. He finished the bread and cheese in two good bites, and after he had rested he kept the berries in his hand to munch as he walked slowly along. They were sour and good for thirsty mouths, which was just as well, since the auntie who had sent him off in such a hurry had for- gotten to provide him with a water-bottle.

He tried not to think about being thirsty. There was nothing he could do about it. There were no springs or rivers at this side of the Valley, which lay, as wide and flat as a plate, tilted ever so gently up to the jagged rim of the western mountains towards which he was walking, mountains which joined hands with other mountains to form an impenetrable circle around their

4

home.

The only notable feature in the great wide plain was the mesa, its cliffs rising sheer to its flat top and the mysterious Thing. The only water was the river which fell from the mountains to the north, widened into the lake, and then vanished into the Place of the Wall. He ate another berry and told himself that he was not really thirsty. He would not think about water. He would think about his water-wheel...

Jody jogged on towards the westward rim of the Valley. The inside of his mouth felt gummy with thirst, and the constant wind that swept down out of the mountains had dried his lips to horn. Cautiously he licked them. Ow! Already a crack. He touched it with his finger and smeared blood. But thirst or not, he had done what he intended to. He had reached the end of the high grass before the others.

He had reasoned, back at the river, before even the old auntie had stopped scolding him, that he could never catch up with the Fourths, but that the noise they made, ranging to and fro through the long grass in their search for snares, would disturb any game that might still be lingering in the dry Valley. He gathered a dozen smooth round stones, slung them loosely in his kerchief and tucked the knot into his belt. Then he squatted on a smooth rocky place where his foot would not catch in an unexpected tussock. He fitted the first stone into the soft leather cradle of his sling, and waited.

Time had no particular meaning on Isis, except for the scolding kitchen aunties. Time was light and dark. Time was the hunger before a meal. Time was the distance between the longest and the shortest day, between the time of feasting and the time of going without. Jody squatted peacefully on his rock, his clothes blending into the reddish-purple of the stone, his eyes and teeth whitely contrasted against his dark skin. Time passed, and nothing moved but Jody's shadow as Ra swung over towards the western mountains.

As the grass at the edge of the Valley began to tremble he was on his feet. The sling whirled with a noise higher and shriller than the wind, and the first stone flew faster then the eye could follow. It caught a purple-fur squarely on the side of its head. It rolled over and lay on its back, paws curled against the pale mauve of its stomach, a tiny trickle of blood vanishing into the

5

red rock.

Out of the grass burst others, rock-bunnies, stilt-legs, more purple-furs. He whirled, aimed, threw, reloaded, whirled, aimed and threw with a breathless mindless precision, until the kerchief at his belt was empty of stones and the grassland was quiet. Only then did he spare a glance for his catch.

Three purple-furs, all of them as plump as could be expected in the spring, and two rock-bunnies, long-eared, short-tailed: delicious roasted on a spit. They seemed to be quite dead, but he expertly broke their necks to save them possible pain, and stowed them in the grass bag the auntie had given him. It was so full that he could hardly draw the string at its neck, and had to leave a rock-bunny's head poking out, ears high, a comical expression of surprise on its face.

As he swung the heavy load to his shoulder a young roan-buck stepped cautiously out of the long grass. Its coat shone in the afternoon light and its nose twitched moistly as it caught Jody's scent. He was glad that he had only a sling, and had not brought a spear or a bow and arrows. He was glad that his game-bag was full. Deeply happy, he watched the buck step delicately past him, its tiny shining hooves picking their way unerringly between the tussocks of wiry blue-grass and across the shale.

The buck leapt from rock to rock, moving steadily upward towards one of the mountain passes that scalloped the horizon between the high peaks. Jody watched it until its roan coat was lost among the red and purple shadows, and he frowned. That was another of the puzzles of Isis: that the animals seemed able to move over the mountains from valley to valley, while the people could not.

Up there, where the buck had vanished, the air was so thin that a man would become dizzy and faint, and he might, if he were not brought quickly down to the Valley, go swiftly to That Old Woman, the Ugly One. He had never tested the truth of the story, nor had anybody else, since the mountains were taboo. But he couldn't help wondering: did a man get sick and die because he broke the taboo? Or had the taboo been put there in the first place because of the mountain sickness?

Long ago, near the Beginning Time, so one of the stories went, the President himself had climbed the heights, not of the mountains, but of the forbidden mesa. It was hard to imagine

6

President Mark London breaking any of the Laws, much less one of the sacred taboos. As for imagining him as a little boy, that was downright impossible.

His own grandfather, the first Jody N'Kumo, had been full of mischief and naughtiness, he had heard, and that *was* possible. For Grandfather was almost beardless and his hair grew in peppercorn clusters even tighter than Jody's, though now it was grey instead of black; and though his body might be crippled his eyes still held a twinkle in their depths, like the twinkle of a small boy up to something interesting.

But President London! The President was tall and straight, with shoulder-length white hair and a glistening beard that swept his chest. *His* eyes never twinkled, and his bushy brows knotted together in a most terrifying frown whenever he was displeased. He frequently frowned when he saw Jody. He was exactly like the picture of the Lord God in the frontispiece of the Holy Book. Sometimes the younger children got the two muddled—God and President London.

So it was hard to imagine the President breaking a taboo, but apparently it had happened once in the Long Ago. He had climbed to the top of Lighthouse Mesa, which was one of the forbidden places. Then the wrath had struck him and he had fallen towards certain death on the rocks that lay splintered about the foot of the mesa. But, so the story went, he had cried out "Save me!" as he fell, and lo, the Guardian of Isis, the Shining One, had suddenly appeared and stretched out his hand, and the President—no, the boy Mark London—had remained frozen in mid-air halfway between the top of the mesa and the sharp screes at the bottom. Then the Guardian had floated up in the air and picked the boy Mark up in his golden arms and flown down to the village with him.

Jody shivered with awe at the memory of the story, even though it was broad daylight, and stories like that only sounded really scary when they were told around the fires in the dark of a winter's night. The south-eastern face of the mesa was close by him now, on his left as he jogged towards home with his warm load of game. Perhaps it was on the very spot where he ran now that the Shining One had appeared.

Thinking so much about taboos and sacred things was scary, and Jody hastily turned his thoughts to the game that bounced heavily on his shoulders as he ran. The purple-furs would go in a stew, he reckoned, flavoured with herbs; and since they were his kill, the skin and bones would be his. The fur, too delicate and soft for clothing, he would give to his mother to cut into thin strips and weave into a bed cover, warm as Ra and as light as the feathers of a lark, for the sharp winter nights. The bones would make tool handles, buttons, buckles, even coarse needles for heavy work, though his mother and sisters-in-law preferred the bones of the large striped trout for most of their sewing needs.

As for the rock-bunnies, they were big enough to roast whole, spitted over a fire; and from their fur he would have his mother make a warm cap with ear-flaps, and a pair of mittens. The winter was hardly ever cold enough for such clothing, and he knew she would stare; but Jody had another dream, a dream that one day he would somehow be able to dodge the taboos and find a way of climbing out of the Valley and seeing for himself exactly what lay behind those high forbidding peaks that surrounded them.

It had never been done. It could not be done, they said, even if it were allowed. Even the top of the Cascades, where Ra's bow danced on the water, was too high for a man to stay for long. But the dream persisted, and through the years of his growing Jody had made his body strong, stronger than any of the others. He swam to and fro across the lake until he was as fast as a fish. He climbed the lower slopes that were not taboo, until his legs were knotted with muscles as hard as the mountains themselves and his sinews were like whipcord.

Bracketed by the Thirds who were married and masters of their own destiny, and by the Fourths, still only children, he lived in his dreams. And the practical side of his mind, the side that had invented the water-wheel, puzzled out ways of capturing the valley air and storing it in flasks like water, and using it to breathe up in the mountains where the air was so thin. Surely it was possible? Something like that must have been done on the long voyage through the sky from Earth—if the stories were true. They must have carried air with them. After all, that was a voyage that wasn't completed in a day, if indeed it had really happened.

Jody ran with his heavy load of game towards the village, his shadow rippling along before him. He turned towards the north to reach the place where the river, pouring down from the Cascades, entered the lake. The stepping stones were close to the place where he had been working on his water-wheel, but there was no time to stop and rescue it now. Ra dropped abruptly behind the western rim of the mountains, and as he balanced from rock to rock across the river he heard the supper bell. Bother it! Now he was going to be in trouble again.

Since the community numbered over eight hundred people there were two dinner times. At the first session sat the elders and the Council, and those women who were Firsts, though of course *they* were not on the Council, and the Seconds and Thirds. At the second session the Fourths ate, helped by those women from among the Thirds who happened to be on kitchen duty that particular day.

When Jody had planned his strategy of crossing the Valley ahead of the Fourths and picking off the game that they disturbed in the long grass, he had entirely forgotten that they did not have to be home for supper until long after he did. In fact, if they *were* late, nothing much would be said. Mealtimes with the Fourths were a brawl anyway, what with little kids running around and people coming and going.

But First Supper was a formal affair. If he could have sneaked into the kitchen and grabbed something to eat on the sly he would have done so; but the cool larders lay to the north of the great dining hall and could only be reached by walking the full length of the room. He gulped, gave his game bag a hitch onto his shoulder, pushed open the door and marched into the room.

Any hope that the Council might be late in sitting, or that everyone would be too busy eating to notice him, faded as the door swung to behind him. The President had just finished what must have been an extra long grace, and the door clicked shut in the small silence that followed his prayer. Everyone looked up. Jody felt three hundred and seventy-eight pairs of eyes on him.

Only one pair mattered. They were steel grey, deeply set under a bushy tangle of white brows, and right down the length of the hall they held him, as if they were a pair of pincers. The President did nothing to break the silence. He raised one bony finger and beckoned, briefly.

9

"Boy." It was an accusation.

"Sir?"

"Are you not a Third?"

"Yes, sir."

"Are not the Thirds privileged to eat with the Firsts and Seconds?"

"Yes, sir."

"You would prefer to eat with the Fourths, perhaps?"

It was a horrible threat. Jody glanced around. Everyone kept their eyes glued to the plate in front of them. Everyone except Grandfather. Grandfather N'Kumo was looking at him. Was that a twinkle in his eye? Meanwhile this catechism could go on all night, while the food cooled on the platters and the resentment against Jody as the cause of it rose thickly enough to cut with a knife. Better to brave it out and get the punishment over with...

"I am very sorry I am late, sir. I went clear across the Valley after purple-furs and rock-bunnies. Got five too, fat ones. The load made me slower than I expected on the way back." He swung the game-bag from his shoulder with a groan and let his body sag with a weariness that was only half make-believe.

There was an interested stir in the silence. No words. No actual movement. Only an inward twitching as the kitchen aunties mentally adjusted the Thanksgiving menu to include the extra bounty.

The President was no fool. In his long stern rule over Isis he had made of women little more than servants; but unless they were pleased they could be the very devil, and their displeasure showed first in the quality of their cooking. Tonight's supper, for instance, a meagre stew of winter vegetables, said as loudly as words that the women were tired out and discouraged at the poor showing that tomorrow's feast was going to make. Five fat animals would make all the difference to their mood, even if not to the actual food going into eight hundred hungry bellies.

He allowed his steely gaze to soften a trifle, and, though he did not smile, his jaw relaxed and he nodded to Jody. "Put your game-bag in the larder and wash quickly, boy. You're a disgrace in a civilized room." He picked up his spoon and began to sup the watery stew, a signal that the others might also begin to eat.

10

Chapter Two

After scrambling through his supper at the farthest end of the great hall, Jody was set to skinning the rock-bunnies and purple-furs and preparing them for the feast. By the time they were lying in dishes of herbs on the stone shelves of the larder, and he had roughly scraped the hides and left them for the women to finish, the stars were out and it was time for evening prayers.

With a sigh Jody washed his hands and put his bloody apron to soak in a tub of cold water outside the kitchen quarters. There was never enough time for the things he wanted to do, but he simply couldn't risk being late again. He'd have to leave his model water-wheel where it was. It wasn't really a problem. He had fastened it securely below the little rock shelf, so it couldn't wash away; and nobody else would touch it. Nobody would ever touch something belonging to another person without a very good reason. It simply wasn't done.

He walked along the neat pebbled path from the kitchen to his home house. It was one of the original houses, built in the Long Ago out of some strange stuff as hard as stone and as white as the winter covering of the far mountains. It was in the front row and faced directly onto the lake, level with the big hall, the hospital and the work-rooms.

As the community had grown from its first tiny beginnings, row after row of houses had been built behind the original ones, mostly simple huts of bamboo lashed together with grass ropes.

The people had made an attempt at building with stone, but it had not been very successful. The ground had shaken, many years ago when he was just a little boy, and the stones had tumbled and killed the people living in one of the stone houses. Isis had shaken again, only four days ago, though not as hard, the old people said, as the time before. Nobody lived in the stone houses now, so it hadn't mattered when the last remaining stones of the abandoned houses had fallen in.

After That Old Woman had taken the family on whom the stones had fallen, President London had declared that stone

11

would no longer be used in building. This bothered Jody. He found himself thinking all sorts of things, like, why had Isis shaken in the first place? And why had the stones fallen like that? Surely there must be a way of gluing the stones together with something, or wedging them in such a way that if the gods under the ground took it into their heads to shrug again the stones would hold tight instead of tumbling apart. But now, because President London had put a taboo on stone-building, there was no use asking questions and nothing he could do about it anyway.

Jody's house was special because Grandfather, and Grandmother too until recently, lived there, and they were Firsts. There was a fireplace in the living room and two rocking chairs as well as the upright chairs, benches and table that all the families had. As Jody arrived, clean but out of breath, Grandfather was picking up the family Bible from the little table beside him. Across the hearth was the empty rocker where Grandmother used to sit, her knobby fingers nimbly knotting a net bag. Grandmother had been frail for many years, but from Ra-up to Ra-down her fingers were never still, making grass bags, fishing nets, bird traps, and knitting socks for the fast-growing children of the settlement. It had been the saddest day in Jody's life when That Old Woman had taken her to her home in the north.

Grandmother had been the President's sister. It was another heaviness that he had to bear, being the grandson of the President's sister. But it wasn't *her* fault. She wasn't a bit like him and Jody had loved her most dearly.

Jody's two elder brothers, Jacob and Benjamin, lived with their wives and babies in the same house; and all of them, even though they were married people with children of their own, did what their parents, Isaac and Ingrid, told them to. When Jody married, his wife would come to live in this house too. It was his home. It would be his for the rest of his life, unless the unlikely of all unlikely things happened and the taboo was lifted so that some of the overcrowded community could look for a new home somewhere else on Isis.

Jody knew that if that ever happened he would be one of the ones to go, come what may. The very thought of it made him tingle with excitement. But it would probably never happen. The Council had been arguing about it for years. The Valley was

12

getting crowded: there was no gainsaying that. And game was in shorter supply every year. But in the end nothing changed, except that the laws got even stricter and the women worked even harder. Surely it hadn't always been like that?

He was lucky to have such a nice home and such good grand-parents and parents. They weren't all like that. Jody settled down on one of the benches and listened as Grandfather began to read.

After the reading and prayers they all went to bed. Since Jody was the only "single" he had a room to himself, which was a delightful luxury. It would be his alone until he was married, or until the babies grew too big for their parents' room, whichever happened first. But for the moment it was his alone. He liked to lie awake at night, listening to the silence. That was the time when most of his ideas and inventions came to him.

He lay now, his hands behind his head, and thought about his water-wheel. What was it for? the auntie had asked. It was a troubling question, one that had kept him awake for several nights. What he needed was something to turn the round-and-round motion of the axle into something else—something useful. For instance, if the axle were rough instead of smooth at the end, and it were pushed up against something else rough, would the other thing move? Or would all the power and move-ment of the water be lost somewhere on the way?

If it *did* work, he could make the movement of the water do all sorts of interesting and useful things. He could make a spin-ning wheel spin faster and smoother. He might even make a machine that would grind the grain into bread flour. Rubbing the grain between two rough stones was exhausting work and took up so much time. Surely everyone would be happy and proud of him if he could invent a way to make life easier for the women?

Jody woke with a start and an idea in his mind that was so real he could touch it. Ra had not yet risen, but he could see the vague outline of his window, the foot of the bed, and the chest beyond it. He threw on his shirt and breeches and slipped bare-foot out of the house.

It was so simple! The end of the axle of the water-wheel

13

should not merely be rough, but *notched*. That was the secret. And there should be another set of notches in the axle of the mill-wheel. Then when the two came together ... but you would have to be sure that they matched exactly or it wouldn't work ... how would you go about getting them to match?

His bare feet left prints in the dew-soaked turf, and the wet prints marked the rocks as he walked up the shoreline of the lake to the place where the river entered it. He had chosen this place after careful thought, because here all the pressure and excitement of the river's journey from the high country was bottled up and squeezed together before spreading out into the calmness of the lake. In miniature it did what the Cascades up at the top of the Valley did, and it was here, in the stony narrows, that he had fastened his model wheel.

He splashed into the water, his eyes searching among the rocks. At first he thought that the wheel had been taken, and he was filled with helpless raging anger. For if it *had* been taken, it could only be on the orders of President London. The auntie was ignorant when she called his model a toy. The President knew better. If he saw it, he would know that it was a machine— or at least the idea, the dream, of a machine. Why were machines bad? It must have been a machine that brought them from Earth.

He clenched his hands into fists and swallowed, while the hot anger rose blood-red behind his eyes. Then his bare foot touched something strange, and he looked down and saw that no one had taken his wheel. No one had even touched it. Only now it was more than half underwater, hidden from sight by the flurry of spume around the stepping stones that crossed the river from east to west.

Jody had fastened his wheel under a miniature cascade, where the river splashed over a small stone shelf. But now the cascade had vanished, and there was only a riffle in the water to show where the shelf had been. What had happened?

He turned and looked back. The grey pre-dawn light flattened everything and wiped out depth, so that it was hard to judge size and distance. But wasn't the lake a little wider? Surely it had spread, during the night, across the short blue-grass at its verge? Only, how was that possible? Where had the extra water come from? The voice of the river had not changed, and there had been no rain for many days.

There was no time to puzzle it out. Though there was still only the suggestion of a green glow on the eastern horizon, it was Thanksgiving Day. The kitchen suddenly erupted into activity like a nest of wild bees. One of the aunties came out with a pail of slops and caught sight of Jody, and from that instant on he was pushed and chivvied from one task to another.

Lunch was a hunk of bread washed down with water and eaten on the run. The dining hall tables were dragged outdoors and benches were set up for the elders and the Council. For the rest, cushions and bed-coverings were spread out over the grass.

An hour before Ra-down the bell was rung. All the people assembled in silence, and the food was ceremoniously carried out and set down on the long tables. There were piles of oatcakes and steaming bowls of barley. There were dishes heaped with the vegetables whose seed, it was said, had been brought from Earth in the Beginning Time. Carrots and turnips and onions thrived on Isis, and there were beans of many kinds and also a local wide-bladed grass, too tough to eat raw, but which could be boiled for greens. The stilt-legs and the roan-bucks had been turned into succulent stews and pies, and the small game, the rock-bunnies and purple-furs, had been roasting on spits since noon and now lay on big earthenware platters, their skins mouth-wateringly brown and glazed with fat.

Jody felt quite faint with hunger. It had been a long winter, and the kitchen aunties had been grudging with their supplies ever since Christmas. But on Thanksgiving Day nothing was held back, and the long tables sagged under the weight of the heaped platters.

By the time everybody had a plate laden with steaming food and had found a place on the grass to sit, Ra had slid down behind the western mountains and the sky had changed to a clear green. Everyone was in party mood. It had been sunny all day and now the evening sky was as clear as a glass of water. It was a good omen for the year ahead. In some years the sky was overcast and the people had not been able to see Earth as the ceremony demanded. Things had gone badly for them in those years. There seemed to be such a delicate balance between Nature and Man. If the ceremonies were not perfect, if something was forgotten or did not go smoothly, then there was bound to be some kind of trouble in the year ahead. It was inevitable.

Jody climbed down the grassy bank and found a place on a big rock close to the lake, as far away as possible from the benches where the elders and the Council sat. Most people sprawled together on the rugs and cushions high on the grassy bank, but as usual he felt more comfortable at a distance.

He was occupied with a leg of rock-bunny, juicy and fat, and was busy licking the grease off his lips and chin between bites when he felt someone close to him. He turned, irritated. It was Tannis Bodnar, a Fourth just one year younger than him, and a greatgrandchild of one of the more influential Council members.

He frowned, intending to show her clearly that she was an immature Fourth, and that he wanted to be left alone to get on with his thinking in peace. Then he remembered the scoldings of the day before, and it occurred to him that he would be less conspicuous if he was not alone at the feast, and that if Tannis was sitting beside him then at least no one else would be likely to bother him. So he quickly changed the frown into a smile. "Hello."

"Hello." She looked at him cautiously and took an enormous bite of the roan-buck pie she held in both hands. "I saw you coming home from hunting yesterday," she went on indistinctly.

He licked his greasy fingers and sopped up the gravy with a flat piece of bread. "I suppose everyone did," he said gloomily.

She giggled. "Was the President furious with you for being late? Why are you always late for things, Jody? Some of the other Fourths say that you're touched in your head, but I don't think that's so. After all, you did kill five animals with your sling, just like that . . . so they say. Did you really?"

Jody nodded and swallowed the piece of bread almost unchewed. "I've worked out a way of aiming and letting go at just the right instant. It's all a matter of judgement. But really a sling is awfully inefficient. There's got to be a better way."

"I expect you'll think of it. You think of everything, don't you?"

Jody shrugged modestly. "I do have a lot of ideas, but then,

16

what's the use? Nobody listens."

"*I* would."

Jody stared at her. He had never really noticed her before. She was a very pretty girl, with black hair in two very long plaits, and brown eyes, very big in a face dusted with freckles. Her blatant admiration warmed him inside. He stuffed another juicy collop of roast meat into his mouth and began to tell her about all the ideas he had had, ideas that had come to nothing because nobody had cared. She listened to him, her eyes wide with admiration, looking down only for more food.

Around them the other eight hundred and twenty-seven inhabitants of Isis ate and drank and laughed, filling the bellies that had shrunk during the long winter's fast until they could feel the skin stretch and hurt. As they ate, Ra's light faded and the sky slowly darkened from green to the blackness of deep space.

Voices became lower. Conversations trailed off unfinished. Greasy mouths and fingers were wiped. Every eye was fixed on the western horizon, as the stars slowly popped out of the darkness like fireflies.

The western rim of the mountains that enclosed the Valley hid the true horizon, but there was a cleft between two peaks, like a child's toothless gap; and it was on this gap that every eye was fixed. Two stars appeared close together, white, not very bright. The people watched in silence. At length, as it grew even darker, a third star appeared, making a small triangle point down in the gap between the far peaks. Earth! There was a cheer from everyone but the babies, who had long ago fallen asleep on the grass, glutted with food.

Earth! Small, reddish-gold, quite insignificant in a sky that was by now fully jewelled in magnificence. Jody stared up at the tiny point of light. Could it really be true that his very own grandparents, and all the other Councillors and elders, had travelled through the unknowable emptinesses of dark space from that tiny point of light? Could that poor weak dot of light really have been a place to live, a place called Home? Of all the legends and stories that the Council told, even the ones about the Guardian, this one was the hardest to swallow.

Under cover of the President's speech, which was the same as the one he had given last year and the year before and for as long as Jody could remember, and which he would probably go on giving until the end of time, Jody whispered to Tannis. "Do you really believe that *we* came from that little dot in the sky?"

Tannis didn't answer him, but she clapped both her hands over her mouth, whether to stifle a giggle or a cry he couldn't tell. Above her hands her eyes shone in the dark as she stared at him with a sort of scandalised admiration.

The speech droned on. ". . . and so we once more celebrate the day upon which Pegasus Two landed on Isis, the day upon which our settlement was founded . . ."

"Can't hear a word he says," snapped one of the very old aunties in the querulous carrying voice of the deaf. "What is he saying, boy?" She looked down from the grassy bank at Tannis and Jody.

He whispered to her. "The same as he said last year, auntie."

"And the year before," Tannis added, but in a smaller whisper for Jody's ears only. Then she put her hands over her mouth again and he felt her shoulders shake.

"So it should be." The old woman peered down at them short-sightedly. "No call to be changing words. That's what ceremony is all about—words and actions you can count on. But nothing else is the same these days. I remember when I was a little girl, smaller than that silly child there, the President used to talk into a little box and his words came out like thunder, so that you could hear them clear across the lake. That was the last President, not this one. Things have changed and not for the better. There's no sense in it all that I can see. But at least the ceremony is the same, thanks be."

Then one of her neighbours nudged her, and her words faded into a background rumble of discontent no louder than the sound of the night wind in the long grass and the river coming down from the high country.

The speech drew to its familiar end ". . . and we thank you, Guardian, Shining One, for your protection. Keep us always in your memory. Send us warning of the wrath of Ra, so that we may seek shelter from it. And keep us always in your hands."

There was silence, and then a whispered "Amen" came from the eight hundred throats of the assembled people, to be wafted away on the cool night wind.

The next part of the ceremony was the choosing of the

Bearers. They were picked, four young men each year, from among the unmarried youths, and therefore, in recent years, from the Fourths. They were chosen by lot, and it was not considered chance, but the hand of the Guardian, that influenced the choice.

Jody had his doubts about that. It seemed to him that the lot fell most frequently on the best behaved, or on those whose ancestors were most in favour with the President in that particular year; and he believed that the Guardian had very little to do with it at all. After all, why should a Being whose task it was to keep Ra rolling around Isis, and the stars in their places in the sky, concern himself with so paltry a matter as the drawing of lots?

He sat gazing out at the dark lake, idly watching the reflections of the stars in the water, and paying little attention to what was going on. The water *was* deeper, he was sure of it. It was much closer than before to the trunks of the fruit trees that grew on the far shore. Over there the slope from the water was more gentle than at the eastern shore where the village was built.

Tannis suddenly screeched and shoved him so hard that he nearly fell off his rocky perch. "Jody, it's you! You're one of the Bearers. They're calling for *you!*"

He stared blankly at her, his mind far away. "What?"

"Go on. Hurry!" She pushed him. The word was taken up by those sitting close by.

"Get a move on, Jody."

"Bad enough to be late for dinner, but to keep the Guardian waiting. . . !"

Jody scrambled down off the rock and picked his way up the bank between the seated people. He made his way up to the square in front of the dining hall where the flag fluttered noisily in the evening wind. The other three Bearers were already washed and dressed in their robes of ceremonial white. He was pushed and pummelled, his face and hands scrubbed with startlingly cold water, and his robe thrown over his head. Someone was still twitching it into place when another hand thrust a lighted torch into his left hand and he was pushed into place.

The President stared wordlessly at him, but his exasperated sigh was audible to everyone around. He dipped a resin-coated torch into the fire and raised it above his white head. "Let us

19

now bear our thank-offerings to the Shining One, and ask him to grant us a good harvest, fine hunting and healthy babies." The torch held high, the President began to walk with slow dignified tread along the river bank towards the Cascades.

The four Bearers stooped to lift the litter with their free hands and fell into place behind him. The litter was quite light, made of evenly matched lengths of bamboo, bound together with the braided fibres from the sword plant, and painted gaily in the reds and purples that were obtained from the local rocks. It was laden with a roast rock-bunny on a platter covered with grass and decorated with berries, a deep bowl of cooked wheat mixed with winter-berries and sweetened with wild honey, a flat loaf of bread, and a big dish of the best of the dried fruits and nuts.

It wasn't a particularly heavy burden for four healthy boys, but it was difficult to keep their rhythm as the trail became rougher. Whenever they had to break step to scramble over a rock or dodge a pot-hole, the litter bounced and wobbled. Once a pepper-nut fell off the pile, but Jody nimbly caught it and popped it back. Nobody seemed to notice except Bob Holmstrom, who was holding the right back corner of the litter. He let out a giggle like a small explosion, which he hastily turned into a sneeze.

Not that it was noticed. The whole community, streaming along the path behind them with torches flaring wildly in the strong north wind, were bellowing the sacred songs as loudly as they could.

Under cover of the noise Bob whispered, "What took you so long? Is it true that you were with a *girl*?"

"Yes. I mean no. Not like that. I was thinking of something else, that's all, and I didn't hear my name called."

"You're strange, Jody. A chance to bear the sacred litter, and you don't *hear*!"

"It's not the most important thing on Isis," Jody whispered back, goaded past endurance.

"Not the most important..? You *are* crazy! If we live through it we're going to be lucky for the rest of our lives. We get our pick of the girls. We'll stand a much better chance of being on Council when our turn comes."

"What's so special about that?"

"Well, I for one would like to sit at the head table and get first dip into the food platters. And I'd rather tell people what to do, instead of always being the one who gets told," Bob answered in a scornful whisper.

They became silent as they reached the bottom of the Cascades, where the President already stood facing the crowd, his ceremonial robe fluttering, the wind blowing his hair and beard and the smoke from the torch that he held high above his head.

The singing died away, and then there was no sound except for the overwhelming noise of the water pounding on the rocks at the foot of the triple waterfall. The procession had stopped, so that, looking back, Jody could see a solid line of fire winding back along the narrow part of the valley towards the village.

The four Bearers moved cautiously forward. It took all the cunning they could muster to keep their footing on rocks that were smooth and slicked over with blown spray. But even as Jody's brain told him where to put each foot next and how to balance his weight to compensate for the tilt of the rocks and the force of the wind, all the time he was doing this, part of his mind was turning over what Bob had said. He realised that although he didn't want to go on being a nobody in the community for the rest of his life, he didn't really want to be on the Council either. Why? The question nagged at him as he and Bob and the other two boys moved cautiously, crab-like, ever closer to the smashing arc of water.

Was it because the Council really didn't *do* anything? Their role seemed to be to make sure that everybody went on doing exactly what they had done the year before, and all the years before that. The idea was that if things had gone well then obviously nothing should be changed. If things had gone ill then it was probably because someone had broken one of the many taboos that enmeshed the most ordinary of actions. In any case a change would probably make things worse the next year. That was the way the Council seemed to think.

The Bearers were so close to the falls now that the force of the water made its own wind, threatening to pull them downwards, pounding against their ears. From now on the danger was extreme. Jody's was the most dangerous position. Holding the left back corner of the litter, he was at all times the closest to the drop, and if the leading two should move suddenly, or turn

21

inward too closely to the wall of rock, it would be he who would be swept out and down into the terror of pounding water and toothlike jagged rocks.

He made his mind empty of everything except the knowledge of what he must do. The main flow of the river pushed outwards over a knife-edge of rock far above their heads at the top of the Cascades, and here, close to the bottom, a hollow space had been worn, as big as a very small room, right under the falls themselves. In there was the Room of the Offering. In there they must leave the litter of food.

Toe by toe they moved forward across the soaking rock. The leading two boys vanished beneath a curtain of spray. Jody glanced quickly at Bob. His face was grey and drawn with fear and the hand that held the torch trembled. If he were to panic or slip now they would both go over...

"You'll make the Council, Bob," he whispered, as they edged towards the curtain of water, and he saw the responsive grin, the lessening of tension. Jody found himself holding his breath as they ducked under the water, but in fact the spray curtain was thin, and behind it the air was breathable, though very damp.

They were in the Room of the Offering. Carefully, very slowly, they bent their knees to lower their burden to the floor. Then, as carefully, they stood upright again, their torches dimming and flaring in the chancy air currents.

Water streamed from the back wall and ran darkly across the floor to join the solid wall of white that screened the small room. Jody found himself looking into the white fall of water. It seemed almost solid, and yet you could see the continual movement downward, ever downward. It was restful to watch it, to let one's body follow one's eyes, to lean forward, outward, downward.

Jody started and pulled himself together. He could see the other three standing like dark statues in the same trance-like state. He called their names, his voice hollow, deadened by the overpowering thunder of the water above their heads. But it was enough. Each of them heard him, started, came to himself.

They stared at each other. This moment they shared, as they stood so close to death that they could feel the breath of That Old Woman chill on their faces, was something that they would never share with another human being. It drew them together in a bond as strong as love. They smiled at each other. They had made it! So far, at least...

It was not always so. Every so often the Guardian reached out his hand and claimed one of the Bearers as his price to be paid to the Ugly One. This was to be expected. That Old Woman was sometimes greedy, sometimes easily satisfied. From year to year there was no telling.

One terrible year a Bearer had slipped on the way into the Room of the Offering. His friend had unthinkingly reached out a hand to help him, and somehow, none of them could afterwards explain just how it had happened, the litter had tilted, slipped, caught in the tearing weight of water, and been twisted out of their hands, to be pounded to pieces on the rocks below, the Offering lost for ever.

That year had been very bad. There was nothing in the history of the people of Isis to tell them how to cope with such a rejection by the Guardian. They were much afraid, and it seemed that that year nothing went right.

The following Thanksgiving Day, just after the offering had been placed with even more than usual care on the floor of the Room of the Offering, the young man who had held the left back corner of the litter, the same position that had been held by the boy who had slipped the year before and caused the whole catastrophe, had twisted his bare foot on a loose piece of scree and had pitched, with startling suddenness, right through the white curtain of water to his death in the darkness among the rocks below.

The people, who had seen his body hurtle through the air almost as if he were flying, comforted his sorrowing family and went home with the happy assurance that the Guardian was no longer angry with them. He had accepted a sacrifice in lieu of the lost offering of the year before, and now all would be well.

And so it was. That year, the winter was unusually short, it seemed, and none of the elders or Councillors died. Indeed, they told each other, well satisfied, when the Guardian spoke it was with a loud clear voice.

So now the Bearers of this year's thank-offering grinned a little self-consciously at each other, and carefully, *very* carefully, since none of them wished to be sacrificed to the wrath of the Guardian unless it was absolutely necessary, they turned and retraced their steps across the swimming floor, under the curtain of spray, onto the slippery rocks at the side of the triple waterfall.

Once outside, the light of eight hundred flaring torches turned the night into a strangely golden day. Jody blinked at the dazzle after the gloom of the cave.

As each boy climbed carefully down and reached the safety of the river-bank he held his arms above his head in the traditional gesture of success, and the crowd roared. Four times they roared, and then, torch flames tossing and guttering in the wind, the crowd slowly turned and made its way back to the village. Now it was time to put the small sleepy children to bed and then, each in his own house, the others would gather around to listen to the family history over a mug of mulled wine and a dish of Thanksgiving Day honey-cakes.

As the crowd turned and surged towards home, Jody found himself standing close to the President. He would liked to have pretended that he hadn't seen him, but in spite of himself Jody found his eyes drawn to that stern face, austere and craggier than usual in the alternate light and shadow of the torchlight.

The President was staring straight at him, his cold grey eyes seeming to pierce Jody's soul. For just an instant Jody thought he saw a bright flare of anger in those eyes, and he felt sure that the President was wishing that he *had* been taken by the Guardian as a sacrifice to That Old Woman: that indeed was why he, Jody, had been picked as a Bearer in the first place. He told himself, as he stared back, unable to look away, that it must be his imagination, that after all what could the future of one insignificant boy matter to the President of Isis?

Chapter Three

Jody went to sleep, his head spinning with strong mulled wine and Grandfather's story-telling, and he did not wake up until Ra was high above the eastern mountains, turning the smooth waters of the lake into molten silver. In fact it was that light, shining fiercely into his room, which awakened him.

All the extraordinary events of yesterday rushed into his mind, and he sat up abruptly, his heart beating hard. There had been the feast, then being picked as one of the Bearers, his brand new idea about the water-wheel. That made him remember the lake and the puzzle about the rising water. Was it still spreading wider and wider across the Valley? Or would everything be back to normal this morning?

It was very quiet. It seemed that no one else was awake yet. Unpleasantly aware of dizziness and a mouth that felt like dry sand, Jody pulled on shirt and breeches and crept out of the sleeping house.

The streets were deserted. Earth's flag still hung, no longer bravely waving, but heavy, drenched with dew, at the flag-pole in front of the dining hall. The grass was wet too, and as the fierce heat of Ra touched the cold ground, the moisture smoked upwards in tendrils of mist. Mist too lay softly over the surface of the lake, blurring its outlines.

Was it any deeper? He walked slowly towards the place where the river entered the lake. His water-wheel was now almost entirely submerged. The level of water must have risen a full hand's span since he had first placed his model under the miniature waterfall. Had the Council noticed? If not, he supposed he would have to tell them . . . or perhaps he would tell Grandfather and see what he had to say. But not yet. He would get short shrift if he wakened anybody on the morning after Thanksgiving; and there was no sign of life in any of the sleeping houses.

Looking back into the sunlight made the dull ache behind his eyes worse, and his mouth still felt like dust. He walked bare-footed up river to where the Cascades thundered, and after bowing down and praying to the Guardian of Isis he took off his clothes and plunged into the water that frothed and bubbled out of the pool below the waterfall.

It was like being skinned with icy knives. He let out a yell of surprise, but his voice was swallowed up in the deeper voice of the falls. He fought his way upstream against the current, and soon he was no longer aware of the coldness, as the river swirled and bubbled and beat against his skin. He felt alive, wonderful. His headache vanished, and he scooped up mouthfuls of sweet, icy water to quench his thirst.

Finally, weak-kneed from the pounding of the water, he struggled to the shore and pulled himself up onto the warm rock, shaking the drips from his hair. Then he collapsed onto his stomach and let the warmth of Ra knead his tired muscles and relax him into a delightful half-sleep.

After a time he rolled over onto his back and gazed up at the sky. The Cascades were behind his head, his feet pointing towards the village, and as he watched the water thunder down towards him it seemed at first as if the whole planet were falling on him. He felt as if he were being battered thinner and thinner and smaller and smaller until he was nothing more than a single thread in the fabric of Isis.

Then suddenly it seemed that the pure green of the sky was an enormous meadow through which he was running, and the waterfall a tremendous fountain that gushed upward from it. He watched, entranced by this new perspective, until an eagle swooped down ... or was it up? ... out of the eastern mountains, and he felt the world swing dizzily back to normal. The green beneath his feet became the nothingness of space and sky again, and the earth rocked and then settled solidly once more beneath his head and spine.

The eagle soared above the Cascades, enjoying some invisible updraught. Jody's eye followed it as it circled slowly, lazily. He caught a flash of colour up at the top of the Cascades. A colour that did not feel *right*, that did not belong to Isis.

He sat up abruptly and turned, hugging his knees for balance, looking up, past the triple falls, past the wind-flung spray to the sharp edge of rock over which the river poured. Had he imagined that flash of brilliant colour? No, there it was again. An instant's glimpse of red, a tag of something soft that fluttered in the wind.

What could it be? And how had it got there, past the reach of the people of Isis? He scrambled to his feet and put on his shirt and breeches, ready to run back to the village and tell everyone of his amazing discovery.

Then he stopped. He turned and looked upward again. *Was* the cliff climbable? There were rough ledges, almost like steps, over there to the right. Suppose he were to climb up and fetch the thing down. *Take* it to the Council. What a triumph that would be! They would hardly be able to go on thinking him of no account then.

On the other hand the Cascades were sacred to the Guardian; and in some inexplicable way they marked the northern limits of the people. They were not precisely taboo, as the mesa and the mountains were, nor as the Sacred Cave and the Place of the Wall. But they *were* holy.

The words that every child on Isis first learned came unbidden into his mind: the Valley is yours and the slopes where the rock-bunnies play; further you shall not climb. The river is yours, and the lake; further you shall not swim.

The river is yours and the lake ... The Cascades were certainly part of the river, and the knife-edged rocks over which the water poured was part neither of a mountain nor of the mesa. What would happen to him if he were to climb up there? The rock-bunnies survived, and the eagles flew immeasurably higher, and the tiny larks higher yet.

As he stared upwards, unable to make up his mind what to do, Jody saw the Bow of Ra, painted in the air more brilliantly than he had ever seen it before, an archway of pure colour, gold, green, blue and purple, its left tip hanging in the spray above the falls to his left, its right tip touching the exact spot where the red thing fluttered. The Guardian had sent him a sign, as clearly as if he had spoken aloud.

Without wasting any more time Jody rolled his breeches above the knee, spat on his hands and began to climb. A grown man, tall and in top condition, would have found the climb strenuous enough. To Jody, at that stage in growing when the muscles had not quite caught up with the bones, it was almost impossible. In spite of his self-imposed training he found that rock-climbing used muscles that he had never exercised before.

27

The front of his thighs knotted and cramped. He could feel his knee joints weaken. Twice he stopped, trembling with fatigue, the sweat running into his eyes, and made up his mind to go back. But each time when he looked down the earth swayed beneath him and did its upside-down trick again. To look ahead and climb on seemed to be a less horrible alternative to having to climb down. He did not let himself think of the obvious: that whether from halfway up or three-quarters of the way or from the very top, the awful climb down would have to be made sooner or later.

Gradually he became aware that he was getting cooler, that the sweat was drying on his face. He found that he was climbing up into a wind that poured over the lip of rock just as the water did. He began to smell the spicy fragrance of thorn bushes and the dry upland grass, instead of water and wet rock. Then his fingers, reaching up once more, curled around an edge. He found one more foothold and heaved. He swung his stomach across the rock edge, and rolled, breathless, onto flat ground.

He lay on his back struggling for breath while the sky rocked above him. The air was like a knife in his throat, cold and sharp and painful. He had to work to drive each mouthful of air down into his body, and he could hear his chest wheeze with the effort like an old man's. But after a time the sky stopped swinging, and the wheezing and the weight on his chest became less noticeable, and he was able to sit up and look around him.

He was on a small, flattish col between two great purple mountains that seemed to rush up into infinite space above him, one on either side. He got slowly to his knees and then to his feet, and stood staring towards the north, towards the new Isis, that no man had ever seen. His blood thudded loudly in his ears and he felt dizzy with excitement.

Ahead of him rolled range after range of mountains, their lower slopes hazy with the familiar stubbly blue-grass, their heights razor-sharp in the thin dry air. He tried to trace with his eyes the course of the river, *their* river, towards its source; but after a few twists and turns its silver thread vanished in the tumble of mountains.

He gave up and looked south, down into the Valley where he had been born, the Valley where the people of Isis had lived since the Beginning Time. It was as familiar to him as the lines

28

on the palm of his hand; but now he saw it as never before, as the lofty eagle might see it.

The houses had become rows of small boxes, with the larger box in the centre front which was the dining hall. He looked over towards the west until the cliff face of the mesa, itself still towering above him, cut off the view. He saw the bright green squares, like a patched quilt, where the Earth crops had been planted among the heavy native red-grass.

He looked down at his feet and saw the river plunging giddily down the scarp, pounding furiously into the pool at the bottom—had he really climbed up from those dizzy depths?—and foaming and fussing down its narrow bed, until quite suddenly it widened into the stillness of the lake. He could see a cloud reflected perfectly in the water. From up here it did not even look like water, but like a piece of fallen sky.

His eyes followed the lazy meanders of the river as it looped like a grass-snake across the marsh that lay to the south of the village. Past bamboo and marsh grasses it wandered, to vanish abruptly under the archway in the Place of the Wall. Jody quickly shut his eyes and turned away.

The Wall. It was white and hard and high, more than twice the height of a man, and it was made of that strange substance of which the first houses had been made. It enclosed an area almost as large as the village. In it was not a single crack or gap. There was only the low arch in its northern side that spanned the river and swallowed it up. The river flowed under the arch. It had flowed so since the Beginning Time when the Wall was built. But why the Wall had been built no one ever said, and what happened to the river after it entered the Place of the Wall no one knew. But the Wall was taboo. The Place behind it was taboo. Even talking about it was taboo.

So when Jody's eyes, wandering curiously down the Valley in this new eagle-view of looking, saw the Place of the Wall from above, so that, if he had gone on looking, its whole circle would have become visible to him, like a dish, with whatever lay inside it exposed to his gaze, he shut his eyes at once, crossed his fingers for luck and muttered a prayer to the Shining One. And when he opened his eyes again he was very careful not to look in that direction, but to keep his eyes on that part of the Valley that was directly below the Cascades.

29

It was only then that he remembered the thing that had challenged him to climb up to these heights. He looked around him. It was over to the left, a long red cloth fluttering in the downdraught from the mountains, tied firmly to a stick which had been pushed into the stony ground close to the precipitous edge of the col.

He untied the cloth and pulled it between his hands, wondering what it could be. It was made of a strange slippery stuff, nothing like animal hair or plant fibre, and it was so finely woven that he could hardly see the separate threads. He had thought at first that it was a piece of rag, torn from a wider cloth, but on close inspection he could see that it had been woven that way, no wider than half a handspan. Why would anyone wish to do such intricate work, which must have taken tens of days? And what was it for?

After he had looked at it for a while the idea began to form in his mind that perhaps the cloth, beautiful though it was, was not the important thing. Perhaps its brilliant red, brighter than any of the dyes that the women of Isis could extract from plants and lichens, was only a signal to catch the attention. Perhaps the message was in the stick to which the cloth had been fastened; or, if not in the stick, even beyond there.

He pulled it with some difficulty out of the hard ground. It was a marking stake, that was evident, but different from any he had ever seen before, as the cloth was different from any cloth. Its pointed end was of metal, sharp enough to be a spear, and the rest of it was square in shape. It reached waist high when its point was on the ground, and it was painted in stripes of black and white. The stripes were a little narrower than the width of his little finger, and on each white section was a black number, and on each black section a white one. At the bottom, close to the spike, the numbers began with 1, and they went on upwards past 10, which was the last number Jody knew properly. About halfway up the stake, where the number was a 4 and a 5 together, the black sections changed to bright red.

It was very beautiful, more perfectly made than anything Jody knew. It was not wood nor metal, apart from the spike, nor was it made of bone or stone. It was very hard, and as smooth as a freshly caught fish; and what was the purpose of it he had no idea in the world. Who could have placed it up here at

30

the top of the Cascades, where no man came? Where had it come from?

He turned it over and over in his hands. This wonderful thing must be shown to the President and the Council at once, and *they* must decide what it was and what it was for. Showing them this new thing would be an excellent excuse for approaching them about the rising level of the lake.

Jody was now faced with the seemingly impossible task of climbing down the way he had climbed up, only now he would have one hand occupied in carrying the stick. He thought for an instant of tossing the stick down ahead of him, but suppose it were to break or be lost in the churning waters of the pool? But to climb one-handed . . .

In the end he tied the stick rather awkwardly to his back above his hips, using the red cloth. He hoped that the projecting ends would not catch in anything on the way down. The drop looked awful. He crouched and peered over the edge, searching for the best route. The idea of having to turn around and dangle his legs above the abyss made his stomach churn. Yet obviously that was the only way to get down. He felt suddenly cold and short of breath again. Maybe there *was* less air up here than in the Valley. Maybe if he stayed up here too long he would stop breathing and That Old Woman would take him. On the other hand, if he slipped on the way down he certainly *would* die, or be crippled for the rest of his life like Grandfather, and that would be far, far worse.

Directly below the place where the stake had been jammed into the ground there was a route that looked a shade less terrifying than any other. Could the person who had planted the stake have known that? Was it an omen, as the Bow of Ra had seemed like an omen?

Without giving himself any more time to think, Jody said a swift prayer to the Guardian to keep him from falling, and then slid around on his stomach, feeling for footholds with his bare toes. After he had swallowed the fright that jumped up into his throat as he hung over the edge, he found it was not too bad. This route had most certainly been used before. In one place there was a metal spike driven into the rock just where his outstretched foot needed it. In other places the rock had been hollowed into hand-holds and steps, by some magic hand it

31

seemed, since there were no chisel marks and the rock was as smooth as if it had been glazed.

He climbed slowly down, trying not to think overmuch, and it was a shock when his reaching foot suddenly touched solid ground. He whispered a word of thanks to the Shining One, unhitched the stick from its uncomfortable harness across his back, and ran as fast as his wobbling legs would carry him back to the village.

First Breakfast was nearly over, and the Fourths were milling around, the younger ones playing on the turf, waiting for their mealtime. Jody pushed between them towards the dining hall, opened the door and marched in, the stick held high, the ribbon fluttering from it like a flag.

The door shut behind him with a bang, leaving the hungry Fourths outside. Every eye turned to the door and the conversation was cut like a broken rope. Jody swallowed, and then with his head up he marched the length of the crowded room, the painted stick held high above his head, until he was standing in front of the table where sat the male elders and the Council, the President in the middle of them.

There was complete silence as the cold grey eyes of President London met the guileless brown ones of Jody, grandson of his old enemy. In that silence it seemed to Jody that the anger of the whole community hung above him, ready to break over his head like a rockfall.

The spell was broken by old Pete McCann, the oldest survivor of the elders, who reached out a gnarled hand and took the stick. "It's like ... like one of our old survey stakes," he muttered, in his wispy voice. He rubbed his hand lovingly up and down the stick, feeling the smoothness of it. "Like ours, but not ours. Theirs." He looked up and Jody saw his eyes meet the President's. It was as if there were a battle between the two of them, a battle without words or movement. Then the elder gave the stick back to Jody and sat, rubbing his finger and thumb together as if he was still absentmindedly relishing the smoothness.

"Where did you find this, boy?" The President's voice broke the silence. Not remembering, or seeming not to remember, the names of people was one of the ways in which the President made himself more important than anyone else on Isis.

32

"At the top of ... of the Cascades." Jody suddenly faltered. The audacity of what he had done hit him, and he felt his knees go loose and trembly. There was a gasp from all the tables within earshot of his muttered words; and then like the wind through the grass at the beginning of a storm, he heard the whispers fly from table to table down the long room.

He told himself that he had done nothing wrong. After all, the Cascades were holy, but they were not taboo, though by the scandalised whispers you would think they were. But he'd done it again, Jody realised, as usual too late to be any use. He had done something DIFFERENT.

He suddenly remembered the time he had flown a kite in a lightning storm. Everybody had accused him then of just wanting to be different, to stand out from the others. Nobody had listened when he had explained that he had just been trying to catch some of the lightning to find out what it was made of. And, after all, he hadn't been badly hurt. When they'd picked him up he only had a bitten tongue. And the rain had very quickly put out the grass fire ...

"Jody!"

He jumped. The President had actually called him by name. And his face, miraculously, didn't look so angry any more. "Yes, sir?" he stammered.

"What made you decide to climb the Cascades this morning of all mornings?"

Jody hesitated. "I did not know that today was a day different from any other," he ventured. The President sighed impatiently and a frown began to form, drawing together the heavy tangle of white eyebrows. Hastily Jody wiped all thought of his water-wheel from his mind and began to tell his story.

When he stopped talking, he wondered if his answer was going to earn him a cuff on the side of the head. But then he saw that whatever he had said had been right, from the President's point of view anyway. Mark London stood up slowly, took the stick from Jody's grasp and held it in his right hand, high above his head. Every eye was on him. There was no sound in the big hall. Everyone waited for him to speak. He looked out at them, silent, lordly. Then: "The Guardian has spoken to us. We gave him our offering and he has given us a gift in return. Our thank offerings are acceptable and the Guardian is pleased with us!"

33

The dining hall was filled with the noise of cheering, and under cover of the tumult Jody tried to slip away to his own place at the far end of the farthest table. But the President saw him move and stopped him.

"No. Sit here. Opposite me. Eat. You have earned it."

Someone shoved a chair behind him. A plate of fat fish was thrust under his nose. As the scent of herbs made his nose twitch and his mouth water Jody forgot to be embarrassed by his dirt and torn clothes. He sat and ate as fast as he could, reaching out for bread to mop up the juices, forgetful of the figure opposite, who never ceased to stare at him as he ate. At the far end of the head table Jody's grandfather saw the President's brooding expression and frowned anxiously, his twisted old hands suddenly clasped together.

When Jody had finished he looked up with a comfortable sigh. The dining hall was silent. The President's eyes were on him. He blushed and wiped the gravy from his mouth with the back of his hand. Then, suddenly reckless, successful and full-stomached, he pointed to the stick, still held in the President's hand, and asked, "What is it for, sir?"

"For? It is not *for* anything. It *is*. It exists. It is a gift from the Guardian. What more should it be?"

The question was obviously not intended to be answered, and Jody, who already had several ideas on the subject, swallowed them and sat silently. The President went on talking. "It is traditional that the person who discovers one of the Guardian's gifts must carry it to the Sacred Cave and keep vigil there."

Jody stared. "Do you mean me, sir?" he asked after a while.

The President sighed impatiently. "Yes, you. I cannot fathom why the Guardian should have picked you of all people for this honour. But then the ways of the Shining One are not our ways. Have you finished eating yet?"

Jody nodded and scrambled to his feet. The President thrust the stick, almost angrily, into Jody's hands and then stalked slowly down the length of the dining hall, motioning Jody to follow him. Jody walked in his footsteps with mixed feelings. Part of him was deeply awed at the role that fate—or the Guardian—had so unexpectedly thrust upon him. Part of him was hard put to not to giggle, especially when they left the dining hall and he could see the expressions on the faces of all the impudent Fourths who had been laughing at him only a short time before.

He forced his face into a fittingly solemn expression and followed the President up the length of the village until they came to the place where the stepping stones made a path across the river. Only then did he venture to speak. "The water is higher yet this morning."

"So?"

"Suppose it goes on rising. It could drown the whole Valley and we could have nowhere to go."

"Do you not believe that the Guardian protects us, boy?"

"Yes, sir. Of course I do."

"I should hope so indeed. You would be a very unfitting Finder of the Gift if it were otherwise."

"But . . ."

"The Guardian will protect us. The water will not go on rising. That is the meaning of the gift. Do you understand?"

"Yes, sir." Jody looked down at the water. It *was* higher. And it would take more than the gift of a piece of coloured stick to convince him otherwise.

He followed the President in silence across the rough turf towards Lighthouse Mesa, towards the two shadowy openings at the foot of its sheer cliffs. As they got closer all the laughter that had bubbled up inside him at the faces of the Fourths was driven away by a breathless excitement and fear.

The Sacred Cave had been made in the Long Ago, in the Beginning Times when the elders had come to Isis from Earth, so the story went. In the Beginning Times, they were told, the people had nothing but the battered ship that had brought them from Earth to protect them from the storms of Isis. So the Guardian, the Shining One, had come among them and taken pity on them in their misery. He had pointed his finger at the solid rock that was the side of the mesa. And, behold, the rocks had melted and a great cave had been formed! And this cave the Guardian gave to the people of Isis to protect them from the storms.

Then he made a second cave, and in it he had placed his holy things, that the people were forbidden to touch. This was the Sacred Cave. It was taboo to all but the President and those

Seconds whose honoured duty it was to keep vigil there in case the Guardian should wish to speak to them.

The Guardian had not spoken for many summers and winters, since long before Jody was born. But still the Seconds kept watch, without food or sleep for a day and a night each, just in case the Guardian should break his long silence. Within the Sacred Cave, too, was the signal that told the people of Isis when a storm was coming; though what the signal was, none of the Seconds would tell, not that anyone, even a child or a grand-child, would ask. To ask what was in the Sacred Cave was taboo.

Towards this awesome place Jody followed the stiff figure of the President. He held the strange stick upright between his hands like a giant candle. With Ra sending their shadows rip-pling ahead of them like enormous stilt-men, they walked across the sliding slopes of scree until they came to the purple wall of the mesa, which rose sheer above their heads to touch the sky.

The entrance to the Sacred Cave was very small, an oblong of darkness in the sunlit wall of the cliff. Its edges were as square as if they had been cut with a ruling stick, and there were grooves in the rock where a door could be slid across to protect whatever it was that lay inside from the dust-storms of Isis.

But now the door stood open, and as soon as they reached it the President stepped across the threshold, moving so quickly from sunlight to shadow that it seemed to Jody's eyes that he had suddenly become invisible.

He himself stood a safe arm's length from the opening, and politely held out the Guardian's gift for the President to take from him. But the President did not take it.

"Come on then, boy. Come." His voice was impatient.

Jody took a hesitating step into the darkness. At first he could see nothing at all, but gradually he became aware of the Presi-dent's long white hair and beard floating, apparently disem-bodied, in front of him. It was a scary sight which did nothing to bolster his failing courage.

He swallowed. "Sir!" His voice echoed strangely. "I am not a Second."

"I know it. In fact before today I would not have wished to acknowledge you even as a Third. The ways of the Guardian are strange indeed—that it should be *you*, of all people..."

"I ... I don't understand."

"How could you? I myself do not understand. But nevertheless it *was* you who found the Gift and brought it to me, and the rest must follow. It is the custom. The finder of the Gift must himself place it in the Cave, and must himself keep the next vigil, and so every year, on the anniversary of the finding."

"You mean me?"

"You." The President's voice was as cold as a winter's night. "Come. Do not dawdle there."

He strode forward through the darkness with Jody at his heels, his heart pounding uncomfortably.

Chapter Four

There was a faint light, and the passage suddenly widened into a small square room. It was very simple, the walls bare, and as the Guardian must have first made them, shiny smooth, with no signs of cutting tools upon them. It was only six paces deep and about as wide, with a ceiling that was high, too high to touch.

Jody looked around him with awed curiosity. The back of the Cave, opposite the entrance passage, was occupied by what looked like a huge storage chest, entirely filled with little boxes, all made of a dark, dull-finished material, with trimmings of shiny white metal that reflected the faint light.

The light was coming from a candle, held high by one of the Seconds. It was Shaun Connelly, whose daughter Debbie was married to Jody's elder brother Jacob, who now came forward to challenge the visitors.

When Uncle Shaun saw the President himself, and Jody's dark face peering over his shoulder, his face dropped with such a comical expression that again Jody felt giggles boiling up inside him. He swallowed until his ears hurt. To giggle inside the Cave would be the ultimate disgrace, a thing that no one would ever forgive him for.

"President London! What on Isis are you doing here? And with that boy!"

"You may well be surprised, Shaun. I too. But the ways of the Guardian, though strange indeed, are not to be questioned. He has brought us another Gift, in return for our Thanks-offering—and it was Jody who discovered it."

"Jody? Does that mean that *he* is to keep the next vigil?"

"You know the custom," the President snapped. He glanced down at Jody. His face in the candle light looked as if it had been chiselled out of stone. There was no kindness in it. Jody allowed himself just one small sigh. It seemed that no one wanted it to be him who had found the Guardian's Gift, wonderful though the Finding was. But did they all have to make it so obvious? He began to wish he had never made the giddy climb to the top of the Cascades.

"Shall I stay to instruct the boy?" Uncle Shaun's voice interrupted his thoughts.

"Yes. Do that," the President replied. He nodded briefly to Uncle Shaun and swept out of the Cave, ignoring Jody completely.

"Whew!" Jody let out his breath in a whistle that echoed around the empty place. Though the Cave was small, voices raised above a whisper reverberated round and round in a strange and distracting way.

"Hsst!" Uncle Shaun frowned at him.

"All right. But don't *you* start. You'd think I'd done something wrong, finding the Gift. I thought that at last they'd be pleased with me. But it isn't so at all. Why does the President hate me so?"

Uncle Shaun sighed and rubbed his nose with a hard, farmer's hand. "I suppose you of all people have the right to know. Part of it is your family history. The President and your grandfather had a disagreement, long ago. It is not your affair, but it is there, and neither of them has forgotten it. The other thing is that although it is a very wonderful thing to receive a Gift from the Shining One, something that may only happen perhaps once or twice in a lifetime, sometimes it . . ."

"Well, what?"

"It is difficult to put into words, especially in this Sacred Place."

"I have to know, Uncle Shaun. After all, I'm part of it now, don't you think?" Jody added.

"I suppose so." Uncle Shaun stroked his beard meditatively.

He still seemed unable to go on about the Gifts. Jody tried to help him. "Are the other Gifts stored in that thing?" He pointed to the great cabinet that filled the back wall.

"Oh, no. That has been there since the Beginning Times." His voice dropped to an even lower whisper. "That is the sacred place from which the Guardian himself used to speak to us."

"You mean it's not just a story? People used to really and truly hear his voice?"

"Oh, yes. It's true enough. But it was a very long time ago. I have never heard it myself."

"And he doesn't speak to us any more?"

"Never."

39

"Do you know why?"

Uncle Shaun sighed. "That was the bad thing that happened in the year after the Shining One gave us one of his Gifts. That was what I meant ... sometimes the Gifts are two-edged. Wait. I will show you something."

Uncle Shaun held the candle high and moved to the left wall of the cave. Against it stood a table, the only piece of furniture apart from the speaking place of the Guardian. It was a beautiful piece of work, intricately carved by old Adid Halabi. It must have stood there for many years, for Great-Uncle Adid had been almost blind, too blind to work, for as long as Jody could remember. But he recognised his work at once. There were a few pieces that he had carved in the Long Ago in different homes in the village.

Upon this table were laid a collection of the strangest looking objects that Jody had ever seen. Not one of them seemed to make any sense. Uncle Shaun pointed to a small black box, trimmed with bright white metal, that even in this cave had not begun to tarnish. "It was in the year that we received that Gift that the Shining One withdrew his voice from us. From that year to this there has been only silence."

"But the Guardian tells us whenever there is going to be a storm so that we can go into the shelter. Everyone knows *that*!"

"I can tell you now, since you found the Gift. There is a light that flashes, up there." Uncle Shaun pointed to the top of the great cabinet, where a small round thing like a single red eye stared down at them.

"Can the Guardian see us with that thing?" Jody asked nervously.

"The Shining One sees all that we do and protects us and helps us when we do what he wishes," Uncle Shaun quoted glibly.

"Yes, I know. But I mean, does he really *see* us?" Jody stared up at the dull red eye, which seemed to be staring down at him accusingly, as if to say: What are you doing in *my* Cave, you miserable Third?

"Goodness, Jody. Must you question everything?" Uncle Shaun stared uneasily up at the round red eye as if he had never thought of it in that way until Jody had suggested it. "Now stop talking and listen for a change. The next two gifts the Guardian

40

sent to us made no trouble at all. In fact we had good harvests in those years and three healthy children were born."

Jody stared at the two objects on the table. They didn't look like anything that could be useful for anything at all. "Please, I don't mean to interrupt, but won't you tell me what they're for?"

"For? They are not *for* anything. They are gifts from the Shining One. Is that not enough?" He sounded just like the President, Jody thought.

"When I get gifts from my family for my birthday I get things like a new leather belt, or a knife or fishing tackle. Not stuff like this..." He put his hand to the table.

Uncle Shaun slapped at him. "Don't touch, boy!"

Jody put his hands behind his back. "Must I not touch because they are taboo?" he asked cunningly. "Or because you say so?"

"Because I say so. And that had better be enough for you."

"Yes, Uncle Shaun. I just wanted to know. Please go on."

The next gift that was shown him was a long wand of silvery white material, like the stuff that was on the windows of the first houses, only you couldn't see through this to what was inside because of the whiteness.

"In the year that gift came to us the light in the Sacred Cave failed." Uncle Shaun's voice was an awed whisper. "It was terrible. I shall never forget that day, because it was I who was keeping watch when it happened. One minute I was sitting on the floor contemplating the bounty of the Guardian, bathed in white light, as bright as Ra's it was, so that it filled this whole cave, with no room for shadows, only it was not hot like Ra..."

"Truly Uncle Shaun? Or is it a story like the elders tell?"

"It is true. There *was* such a thing. It shone from that place up on the ceiling. I was meditating, as I said, and I saw a flicker. I thought at first that it was my eyes. One tires after a whole night's vigil. But then it happened again, and then faster and faster, until I thought my head would burst. Then, all of a sudden, I was in darkness. And the light never shone again."

"What did you do?"

"At first I thought that I had been struck blind. I wondered what I had done to offend the Guardian. It was terrible. I shall never forget that moment. I felt my way out of the Cave and then I knew I had not gone blind, because I could see the dawn on the mountains behind the village."

"So what happened then?"

"I fell on my knees and thanked the Shining One for not making me blind. But it was still a terrible thing, to take away our light. There was a special meeting of the Council to try and find out what we had done wrong that would cause the Guardian to take the light away from us. That was one time ..." Uncle Shaun stopped talking suddenly.

"What? What were you going to say? Tell me, or I'll ask Grandfather. He'll know. He was there."

"No. Don't do that. It is not good to bring sorrow to old men. What I was going to say was, that that was one of the times when your Grandfather and the President quarrelled. They fought so badly that your Grandfather stopped going to Council meetings after that."

"I thought he didn't go when he was crippled in that fall."

"That was not the real reason. They could never get along, those two. The President said that when things went wrong it was all our fault, and we must search until we found out what was causing the Guardian's anger, and then put it right."

"And what did Grandfather say?"

"He said that things like that could happen by chance and that blaming people was wrong."

"I agree with Grandfather." Jody nodded.

"You'd be the only one then. But then you would. You're like him—a troublemaker."

"I just know he's right."

"Is he? Then why is Mark London President, and your grandfather a crippled old man with no voice on Council?"

Jody grew hot with anger. Then he realised that his uncle was trying to take his mind off the Gifts, so he just shrugged and turned back to the table. "So what did you do about the light?"

"We made special candles of rock-bunny fat scented with clove-berries."

"I meant what did you do to find out what made the light stop working?"

"The President said that it was the fault of your Grandfather and he wanted him to be banished from the Valley. But that time the vote went against him."

"I should hope so. As if it could be Grandfather's fault. And it is death to leave the Valley."

"It was a very narrow margin, nothing to boast of."

"You mean that the Council would actually vote to kill a person, a good man like Grandfather?"

"If it were necessary for the sake of the rest of the people. That was the President's argument. But nobody had ever been sent to That Old Woman by the hand of the people, and that was why the vote went against his banishment."

"And that is why the President hates our family?"

"Perhaps, in part. But the rest is in the Beginning Times, and there is no good in talking of such things."

Jody sighed. "Why did I never hear about this before?"

"It was between the Council and the Firsts and Seconds who were at the special meeting. I only tell you now because you were chosen as the Finder of the Gift. But you must never talk of such things outside this place. Do you understand?"

"Yes, Uncle."

"Now hand me the new Gift. This is the fifth. There have only been five Gifts from the Guardian in the history of Isis. Do you understand now why the President is angry and puzzled? It is an exceptional honour to be the Finder of a Gift. And it was *you* who found it. The questioner. The disturber of the peace of Isis. The grandson of Jody N'Kumo! It is a puzzle indeed. What is this fifth Gift telling us? Is it a warning of some calamity that will fall on us unless we can prevent it by doing something that is pleasing to the Shining One? Or is it a sign that he is already pleased with what we do and the ways in which we honour him? Only time will tell."

"I still say that it looks as if it was *for* something," said Jody practically.

"Nonsense. It is a Gift."

"It reminds me a bit of the measuring sticks that the men use to get the lengths of bamboo right for a new house. And it's a bit like the painted sticks that they were supposed to use in the Beginning Time, only I don't understand what for. But I bet if you really asked one of the elders they would remember and tell you."

"You know as well as I do that the elders are too old to make sense. They live in a world of dreams and sleep. It is no good asking them about such things. And the Gift is *nothing* like a measuring stick. It is a Gift, a miraculous thing. Just see how it is made. And it is intended to *be*, not to *do*."

Jody opened his mouth to argue back, and then shut it again. He shrugged. What was the use? They were all deaf anyway.

"I shall leave you now," Uncle Shaun went on. "I have been here for over the allotted time. Someone will come to relieve you at Ra-up tomorrow."

"What am I supposed to do?"

"There you go again, boy, with your doing. Nothing, absolutely nothing. Just be. Meditate. Pray. Be ready for a message from the Guardian, should he break his old silence..."

"What if..."

"But he has not talked to us since before you were born. It is hardly likely that he will choose to break silence today. If the storm signal should flash you will go to the entrance and sound the warning horn which hangs outside. Three times, remember. But do not worry. It is early for storms. Nothing will happen."

Jody nodded. To keep vigil did not seem such a grand thing after all. He watched his uncle hurry across the blue-grassed scrubby edge of the valley and splash across the stepping stones of the ford. The river *was* higher. It wasn't his imagination. Then he turned reluctantly from the warmth of Ra and the bright spring noises of the Valley, and went down the dark passage into the cold gloom of the Cave.

The candle, which Uncle Shaun had set in its stick on the end of the carved table, cast a weak and flickering light that only deepened and solidified the shadows that crowded into the corners of the Cave, and around the high ceiling and the edges of the big cabinet. The shadows moved as if they were thick with spirits.

Jody swallowed and picked up the candlestick and walked slowly around the room, looking very carefully into all the corners. They were all quite empty. He laughed at himself and set the candlestick down again. In the empty middle of the floor was a piece of rush matting, woven in a design of diamonds in grasses that had been dyed yellow and green.

44

He sat cross-legged on the mat and stared up at the red eye in the top of the cabinet. The red eye stared emptily down at him. Once he thought he saw it flicker, as if the eye had winked; but he opened his eyes very wide and the red eye stared steadily back and did not wink again. His eyes slowly shut. His head fell forward on his chest and he dozed.

He woke with a jerk, almost falling over. Had he slept the whole day through? Was it night already? He slipped along the narrow passage to the entrance and was nearly blinded by the white light of Ra full on his face. It was barely noon!

He shivered and stood for a while enjoying the heat on his cold, stiff arms and legs. Then he went reluctantly back inside. If the light *were* to flash, he must be there to see it and give the alarm. Uncle Shaun had said that it was not yet the season for storms. But it was not far off.

He felt his way back out of the light, sunspots dancing in front of his eyes. How dark it seemed after outdoors! He could hardly see anything. There was a jug of water close to the door. He had a good drink from it. It was cold, but it tasted very flat and there was not much of it. Probably the person coming to keep vigil was supposed to bring a fresh jug with him. In all the excitement and the breaking of an established routine it had been forgotten. He sloshed what was left around in the bottom of the jug. He had better keep it for the night. Not use it all up now.

Once he had made up his mind to this and put the jug carefully back out of the way, he began to feel thirsty. And hungry too. Well, there was nothing to be done. His eyes had recovered from the sudden light of Ra. He was not imagining it, it *was* getting darker in here. He glanced up at the table and saw that the candle was guttering, and that there was barely a thumb's width of stub left. Supposedly a new candle would have been brought by the vigil-keeper, along with a jug of fresh water. Unless there was a store. He had another look around, but there was nowhere to hide a bundle of candles.

Very carefully Jody trimmed the wick. That was better. The light burned more brightly and no longer flickered as badly. But nothing could alter the fact that he had to stay in this place for the rest of the day and the whole night with a candle stub no taller than his thumb was wide.

45

There was nothing else that he could burn. There wasn't even a tinder box. He sat and thought about it carefully. By early afternoon the candle would be finished. He watched a little pool of wax collect and run wastefully down one side, and he tried to dam the flow with his finger. Then he sat on the mat and stared up at the white panel that had once, according to Uncle Shaun, filled the room with the brightness of Ra. What could have made the light happen? And why had it stopped?

The longer he stared at the ceiling the more convinced he became that the white stuff he was looking at was just like the stuff from the Beginning Times, the stuff that made the windows of the old houses and the shelves in the hospital. Whatever actually made the light must have come from behind the white stuff.

Without stopping to think whether he ought to, he very carefully put the Guardian's Gifts and the candlestick out of harm's way against the cave wall, and pulled the carved table until it was directly under the white panel. He climbed on the table. It rocked, but only a little. When he reached up he could touch the ceiling easily. There were no pegs or nails in the white thing. It just seemed to stick to the ceiling. He poked at it. Nothing happened. He tried to get his fingers around it, wobbled and nearly fell. The panel popped off into his hands as if by magic, and he only stopped himself from falling by dropping to his knees on the table, clutching the panel to his chest.

Had he damaged anything? "Phew!" The panel looked as good as new. He put it down carefully and got to his feet again. Now he could see a kind of inverted metal trough, shiny, with a white wand suspended along it, a wand as long as his arm. He looked at it. It reminded him of one of the Guardian's gifts. He looked into the corner where he had put the things from the table. It was *exactly* like the Guardian's Gift.

One of those sure serene moments of truth came to him, as it had when he'd found out about the stuff lightning was made of, and when he'd had the idea for the water-wheel. He put up his hands and tugged at the wand, and it came away easily in his hands. It was cold and smooth and weighed very little for its size. He wondered what was inside it.

He climbed carefully off the table and compared the wand with the other, the Gift of the Guardian. He *had* been right. The two might be twins. His heart pounded and his head almost split in two with dangerous new thoughts. Why would the Guardian want to give his people useless gifts? He was not a joker. He was the Protector. Suppose magic wore out. Suppose he sent them new magic to replace the old. Suppose...

He took a shaky breath, picked up the Guardian's gift in hands that trembled a little, and then climbed carefully onto the carved table. He could see the little pieces of metal like springs at the ends of the metal trough. He had to push the wand so that the ends of it pushed against the metal springs. So...

The Cave was flooded with brilliant white light. It was so bright that Jody collapsed to his knees on the table, covering his eyes with his hands. After a while he peeked between his fingers. The light shone steadily down, banishing the shadows. He remembered the cover and climbed back up to push it into place, squinting against the powerful light. Now things were as they had always been.

He put the table back in its proper place against the left wall, and restored the other Gifts to their allotted places. Only now there were but four of them ... and a gap. He looked at the wand he had taken from the ceiling and then substituted it for the other among the Gifts.

The candle burned with a meek pale light that was almost invisible, and he blew it out. Then he sat down in the middle of the floor to think about what he had done and how he was going to explain it to the Council. The longer he thought about it the more impossible it became. The President's stony face arose clearly in Jody's mind. He swallowed and licked his dry lips.

Perhaps he shouldn't say anything at all. The Cave was a place of miracles, was it not? Years and years ago the lights had gone out. Today they had come on again. Nobody would ever need to know that the white wand on the table was not the original Gift but the worn-out magic. Nobody would ask *him* what he had done, because nobody else would ever think of doing anything. If he just kept quiet everything would probably be all right.

Once he had got that cleared out of his mind, Jody started thinking about the Guardian and his Gifts; and about the President and how he had tried to have Jody's grandfather expelled from the Valley.

The President was *wrong*. That was the clearest thought that surfaced in Jody's mind. And the Council and the Seconds and the Thirds were wrong, because all they ever did was to repeat what the President told them.

All of them, Uncle Shaun, the Council, the other Seconds, all thought that the Guardian's Gifts were objects without meaning or consequence. The wand that had made the magic light come back had been given to the people in the same year that the old light had failed. If they had used it then as it was meant to be used... But nobody had believed that it was *for* anything.

So why should not the other Gifts be more than tokens of the Guardian's pleasure or anger? Jody stood up and walked across the Cave, and one by one, very carefully, he picked up the Gifts and looked at them. One of them was a small heavy object that felt as if it was meant to be held in the hand and looked as if it might be a tool or a weapon. He could not tell why he knew this. But he knew and put it down again carefully, in case he should do something wrong.

The next Gift was a book. That was clear. It was about the size of the family Bible, but when Jody looked inside he didn't recognize any of the letters. They didn't look like the alpahabet at all. Jody couldn't read; neither could any other of the Thirds or Fourths, but he knew what words looked like. And these didn't. They were wiggly, like little worms, and were in odd patterns over the page. There weren't even any pictures, as there were in Grandfather's Bible.

The fourth object was the black box with shiny metal pieces that he had noticed when Uncle Shaun had first shown him the Gifts. He had noticed it then because it reminded him of something, but he couldn't think what it was. He stared blankly round the empty room, and his eye caught the cabinet, clearly detailed now in the strong white light pouring down from the ceiling.

Of course it was familiar! The cabinet was made of tens and tens of little boxes, just like the one on the table. The box, he remembered, had been the Guardian's Gift in the year in which he had ceased to speak to them. Suppose the Guardian needed the help of the box to make his voice come? Suppose this box was intended to replace the one in which the magic had worn

48

out, just as the white wand had replaced the other . . .

But when he took it to the cabinet his heart sank. There were so many boxes and they all seemed to be exactly alike. There was no way in which he could tell which was the worn-out magic. Perhaps it was as well. He put the box back on the table. After all, he told himself, *two* miracles in one day would be a little hard for the people to swallow. At least he knew that he was right. The Guardian was a logical being, and his Gifts had meaning.

He sat cross-legged on the mat. It was easy to stay awake now that the light shone on him, bright and steady. He prayed to the Shining One and thanked him for putting the idea into his head to change the new magic for the old. The night passed slowly. By the time dawn had come Jody was almost convinced that he had had nothing to do with the light. When he heard his replacement scuffling against the loose stones at the entrance he went to meet him. It was Roger London, one of the President's own sons.

"What are you doing out here? You should be keeping watch." Roger frowned. He was a dour self-important man.

"There is a light," Jody found himself blurting out. Before he could say anything more Roger had pushed past him into the cave, moving so fast that the water in the jug he carried sloshed over and splashed on Jody's bare toes.

When Jody followed him back into the Cave he was already kneeling before the black cabinet. He pulled Jody to his knees beside him.

"Do not stand there, boy. Do you not understand that this place is now more sacred than ever?'

"Yes. Yes, of course." Jody stammered.

"When did it happen?"

Jody tried to rearrange his thoughts. He was sleepy and hungry, and what he had done and what the Guardian had done had become by now a muddle in his mind. Where did one leave off and the other begin? "It was the candle," he said at last. "It guttered, and I knew that there would be no other light. I was afraid."

"Wonderful. Wonderful! All these years since the light failed we have brought candles, and the Guardian has held his hand. Last night you would have been in darkness and so the light was restored. How good the Shining One is, who sees all things and knows all things!"

Jody's eyes strayed to the worn-out magic wand that he had taken from the ceiling. Should he say something? He opened his mouth and then shut it again without saying anything at all.

"We must tell my father the good news at once," Uncle Roger said pompously. "I will go at once ... unless ... perhaps the Guardian will give us yet another sign. I will stay here and *you* will go. Quickly. Tell the President everything just as you told me."

Jody jogged thankfully back to the village. He hoped that talking to the President would not take very long. He was *so* hungry. As he splashed across the stepping stones he saw that the level of the lake had risen considerably.

If he could only think of a way of measuring how far the water was spreading each day, would the President permit it? He could ask, while they were still stunned at the news of the light in the Cave. Then the only thing to worry about would be finding a good way of measuring...

Chapter Five

If Jody had thought to surprise the President into thanking him or being pleased with him, he was mistaken. As he explained about the candle guttering and the light appearing, the beetle brows drew together in a terrible frown. When he had finished, and it did not take long to say all he had planned to say, the President waved him away with a preoccupied air. Jody had just turned to go when he remembered about the river and the lake.

He turned back reluctantly. "Sir."

"What is it now?"

"The water, sir. It's still rising. I wondered if you had noticed."

"I am not blind, boy." The piercing eyes savaged him. He hadn't the nerve to say any more, but ran to the kitchen to beg some food, and then, when he had eaten it, he rolled into his bed, his head spinning with tiredness and excitement.

Despite his tiredness he did not sleep well, and he woke in mid afternoon from a dream in which water was rising up to his neck and flowing into his screaming mouth, while a great voice scolded him out of the storm clouds.

The women were busy and shooed him away from the kitchen. The Thirds were all away hunting, and the Fourths were fishing from the small flat boats that they used on the lake. One or two of them waved to him, but he pretended not to see. They would only ask him questions, questions he couldn't answer.

He sat down on a rock that was now lapped by the water at the lake's rim. It had been high and dry ever since Jody could remember. Now the water was right up to it. Was the Council doing anything about it? Were they even talking about it? He was still staring glumly at the water when Tannis came and sat down beside him.

"What are you doing, Jody?"

"Thinking."

"What about?"

He sighed. "Don't you have any work to do?" he countered.

51

"I'm sorry." She slipped meekly off the rock. He should have been warned by that. Tannis wasn't a meek person. But he looked up at her apology and saw her cheeks flushed, her lower lip caught between her teeth, her eyes glistening, and he relented.

"Oh, come on. It's all right. You can stay if you want to." And while she sat, silent now, swinging her short legs, he began to talk about the rising level of the lake, almost more to himself than to her.

As he talked the ideas in his own mind became clearer, so that when he stopped and Tannis asked him, "But where does all the water go to?" the answer jumped unbidden into his mind as if it was something he already knew.

"Perhaps there's a hole in the ground. I don't think I believe in all the stories about monsters or the Hobbit swallowing up the river. I believe the water goes into a hole in the Place behind the Wall."

Jody's own words startled him. Did he really believe that? Tannis said nothing, but both of them looked cautiously down the lake to where the Wall circled about the mystery.

They both felt a chill that had nothing to do with the weather. Ra was at its mid afternoon hottest, and there was not a breath of wind, nor any clouds in the blue-green sky. But both of them suddenly shivered, and both of them turned their eyes away from the high white wall that lay to the south of the village.

After an uneasy silence Tannis said, in a voice made high by pretended casualness, "I wonder what makes places taboo. Do you suppose they were always that way? Even before the Beginning Time?"

Jody cleared his throat. "The Wall is made of the same stuff as the first houses, and maybe it was built when they were. So perhaps before that the place behind the Wall was not taboo. If they brought the stuff for the houses and the Wall from Earth— it is certainly something that we on Isis don't have…"

"But all that's only a story." Tannis suddenly flopped on her back and looked up at the sky through her fingers. "The Wall really is there. But the story about the elders coming from the sky is just make-up. You know that. Why, it's all empty up there. There's nowhere for people to live. Even the clouds are not really solid. They come and go on the wind."

"We're supposed to have come from the stars, you idiot, not out of the sky."

"The stars, you idiot!" she mimicked, suddenly bold. "The stars are only little points of light to decorate the sky at night. A people cannot live on a point of light."

"It is just because they are so far away, don't you see. They are not really points of light. They are suns, just like Ra."

"Even if that were true, doesn't that prove it's nonsense? Nobody could live on Ra. It is far too hot."

Jody frowned. That was a point that had bothered him too. "My grandfather used to say that Earth was a ball of rock that floated around a star, and that Isis floats around Ra the same way."

Tannis caught the doubt in his voice and laughed. "Well, there you are then. Everyone can see that it is Ra that goes around Isis and not the other way about. And does Isis look like a little ball of rock? Your grandfather sounds like the elders, full of crazy stories. And you know we're not supposed to believe *them*. No, anyone can see that Isis is a flat place, like a dish, with mountains all around the edge to stop us falling off into the night."

"Don't you believe that there are other places beyond here? Other valleys?"

"Oh, no."

"When I climbed to the top of the Cascades I saw beyond."

"Oh, Jody! What was there? Darkness and the stars shining?"

"No. There was just more mountains, going on and on. There didn't seem to be an end to them."

"Well, I expect that means that Isis has a very thick rim. But I bet if you went on, in the end you would come to nothingness."

"I wish I could go and see for myself." Jody sighed. "But I can't, because of the taboos."

"Well, of course. You know they are there just to protect us. After all, if we got curious and climbed the mountains we might go too far and fall off the edge into nothingness."

"Do all you Fourths believe that?"

"Of course. It's the truth."

"Well, what about Thanksgiving? When we wait for the Earth star to appear, and then we make the toast: To our Earthly

53

home. What about that?"

"That is just another name for the place in the north that That Old Woman takes us to when we die. Don't you know anything, Jody?"

"Of course I do. It's you who has got it all backwards. Did your elders never talk to you about the Beginning Times?"

"Don't you remember that our family doesn't have any elders of our own? Not that it matters. The President told all us Fourths that though we must be polite to the elders because they are so old, we mustn't pay any attention to their stories about the Old Times. He said that when people become very old they dream about the future world in the north, where they will live when That Old Woman comes for them. And they forget that their dreams are not real and get muddled."

Jody frowned. "They are not the ones who are muddled... I don't think so anyway. And I'll tell you something funny I've been thinking about. Maybe it has to do with not listening to the elders. Things are not getting better on Isis. They're getting worse. And we're not learning more. We're learning less."

Tannis sat up abruptly and stared at him, her mouth open. "Jody!"

"It's true. Look at our houses. The old ones are made of that smooth stuff that never wears out. There are no cracks for the wind to come through in winter, and there are windows that you can see through, and yet the weather does not come in through them. You never have to repair the First houses, the way you do our bamboo ones, every time there's a storm."

"Have you ever tried to put up a new set of shelves in one of the old houses? You can't make a hole in that stuff no matter how long you drill. That's silly."

"Maybe. But the point is, we can't make them now even if we wanted to. And what about light?" He argued recklessly, stung by her indifference to his idea. "Wouldn't you rather have a white light, smooth and steady, coming out of the ceiling, instead of those smelly bunny-fat candles and floats?"

"Well, of course. Who wouldn't? But there isn't such a thing. You just made that up."

"I did not! That's just how it is in the Cave, after I put in the new mag..." He stopped abruptly, hoping she wouldn't notice what he'd said. But she pounced like a mouse on a fat ant.

54

"New mag...? New magic? Is that what you were going to say? The Light in the Cave? That everyone's whispering about? Are you saying that *you* made that happen? Jody, that's crazy!"

"All right. I'm sorry. I just made that up."

"You didn't, though." She stared at his face. "Jody, tell me what you did."

"You know I can't do that. I'm not even supposed to talk about the Cave."

"But you already have."

"That's just because I forgot. I'm not used to the idea yet. But I remember now, so I can't."

"If you don't tell me all about the Cave, then I . . . I'll tell my mother that *you* made the light happen."

"You wouldn't dare," Jody spluttered. But when he looked at her red cheeks and her pouting lips he wondered if she would. "If you did, I would just deny it, that's all. Then *you*'d be in trouble. After all, I'm a Third and you're only a Fourth."

"That's true. But you're Jody N'Kumo, and you're *always* in trouble."

Jody sighed. What was he to do with this exasperating creature? He wished he had never let her sit down and talk to him. "I'm older than you," he tried to persuade her gently. "I'm a Third. I found the Gift and I kept vigil in the Cave. Of course there are things that I know that you do not. It is right and reasonable."

She shook her head obstinately. "I don't care about the other things. You can keep your old secrets. I just want to know how you made the magic light happen."

"Oh, for pity's sake!"

In a whisper, very quickly, he told her what he had done in the Cave. She stared at him with shining eyes. "How brave you are, Jody! I would never have *dared* . . ." Her voice ran up the scale and he shushed her quickly.

"Keep your voice down, Tannis!"

"I'm sorry. I didn't mean . . ."

"Sh! What was that?"

"I didn't hear anything. Jody, why are you so nervous? I won't tell anyone, honestly."

"I should hope not." He shivered suddenly and looked around. There didn't seem to be anyone close enough to hear, and yet he had felt or heard ..."I should never have touched it. I must have been crazy," he muttered.

"You weren't. You were brave. I'm sorry I made you tell me. I wouldn't really have told my mother. Or anybody else."

"*Now* you tell me." He scowled.

"I said I was sorry."

"All right. It's too late now anyway. Would you mind leaving me alone? I want to think and I can't do it with you chattering at me all the time."

This time he didn't look at her, but kept his eyes on the water. He heard her slither off the rock and the scutter of pebbles as she walked away. What was going to happen about the water? It seemed as if the Council would sit and talk, or make up some new story, while the water rose and rose until it was up to their necks.

He needed to make a stick with marks on it and maybe numbers, so that he could see where the water was *now*, and where it would be by Ra-down tonight, and where tomorrow morning. It wasn't until what he needed was clear in his mind that Jody realised that he had "invented" the Guardian's latest Gift. His mouth fell open at the implication. If the Guardian knew they needed a measuring stick, then indeed he knew everything that went on in their Valley, even though he no longer lived among them.

Was the Guardian God? Or was he something more like an angel? It really wasn't very clear. Making the caves by melting the solid rock, holding the boy Mark London in mid-air so that he shouldn't fall to his death on the rocks, telling them of coming storms, these were very God-like things. But then why should he have suddenly left them to muddle along on their own? Unless they had done something bad, and he had abandoned them in anger. There was a story a bit like that in the Bible. About a whole people being drowned in a flood, except for one man and his family and the beasts ...

The dinner bell interrupted his thoughts. He slid off the rock and ran up the slope to the dining hall and wriggled through the crowd to his usual place at the bottom of the furthest table. He kept his eyes fixed on his plate during the President's lengthy prayer, and he ate with concentrated haste, suddenly realising how hungry he was. Once or twice, when he looked up to

56

replenish his goblet or to reach for another piece of bread, he thought that people seemed to be staring at him strangely. But then he thought that it was his imagination, because when he stared back, they just looked past him as if he wasn't there. It was an uncomfortable feeling, and he was glad when the meal was over and they all stood while the President, the Council and the elders filed out of the dining hall.

"Jody!" It was his mother's voice, and at the look on her face he came running.

"What's the matter, mother?" ▪

"Go home at once." She pushed him in the chest to emphasise her words. "Hurry now. Your grandfather wants to talk to you."

"*Grandfather?*"

"You heard."

Grandfather N'Kumo was many years younger than the President, so it was strange that while Mark London was tall and straight-backed, his white hair and beard spreading luxuriantly over his shoulders and chest, Grandfather N'Kumo should be bent and frail. His black face was creased with pain wrinkles, and the peppercorn curls on his head had thinned to a sparse white wool. An accident, many years before Jody's birth, had crippled him, and now, in the eyes of most of the people of Isis, he was like one of the elders—useless, to be honoured and looked after but not to be listened to. The Council of Seven, to which, as one of the male children of the elders, he automatically belonged, seldom saw him and had been for many years the Council of Six.

He spent most of his time sitting in his rocking-chair in the N'Kumo house, and in spite of the presence of his only son Isaac and his daughter-in-law Ingrid, and of his three grandsons Jacob, Benjamin and Jody, and the wives and babies of Jacob and Benjamin, he was often lonely. Since the death of his wife Carrie he was reluctant to talk about the old days. He had drawn away from the other Councillors and the elders, and the old enmity that lay between him and the President had grown into an unscalable wall.

As he sat in the darkening living room, waiting for Ingrid to come in with a light, the old man rocked and rubbed his swollen knuckles, and sighed at the tedious length of his days and at the sweet memories of long ago times which were no more.

When young Jody burst into the room, tumbled and breathless, he felt as if he were looking through a mirror into the past. Not that Jody looked that much like him. Two generations had lightened the N'Kumo skin to a dark brown and thickened the peppercorn hair. But the rangy muscled arms and legs, the wide grin, the lower lip that pushed forward in thought or anger, and the questioning eyes—they were his, the littlest boy on Isis back in the Beginning Time. And dammit, if he'd been young and uncrippled, he would probably have done just what the boy had done, and finished up in the same trouble too...

He sighed, moved painfully in his chair, and gestured with a knobby hand. "Come and sit by me."

"Is something the matter, Grandfather?"

"Why should something have to be the matter for me to want to talk to my favourite grandson..." The old man broke off. "Dammit, Jody! I'm no good at playing games. I'll tell it to you straight. What possessed you to touch anything in the Sacred Cave? What were you thinking of?"

Jody stared blankly. For a moment his mind wouldn't work. Then it filled with a hot anger. Tannis had told! He had trusted her and she had betrayed him. He would have liked to tell Grandfather everything, all the questions to which he could find no answers, his concern about the rising water, what it was like in the Cave when the candle guttered, the magic wand... But now his anger dried up all his words into a hard stone inside him, and all he could do was to shrug his shoulders and stand silently.

"The President is very angry." Grandfather was almost pleading.

"The President is always angry," Jody muttered, but low enough so that though Grandfather heard him, he could pretend that he hadn't.

"Jody, I am so afraid for you." It was unexpected. The cracked voice trembled on the brink of tears. Jody dropped to his knees beside the rocking-chair, startled out of his anger and self-pity. He put his warm hands over his grandfather's cold ones.

"Huh. What can they do?" He said it mockingly, while in the

58

pit of his stomach a butterfly suddenly fluttered. What *could* they do?

"How do I know? No one has ever broken such a taboo before. But the punishment will be bad, worse than you can imagine. Oh, Jody, if it had only not been *you!*"

"You mean, because I'm like you and the President dislikes you so much? Why does he? After all, you were children together, weren't you?"

"Not really. When we came to Isis I was a small child and Mark was almost a man. Then something happened. All I can tell you is that I was part of something that Mark would do anything to forget, something that he has managed to make everyone else forget. But not me. I remember. And as long as I remember the truth, then so must he. It is as simple and as complicated as that."

"What was it about?"

"I cannot tell you even if I wished to, which I do not. But I swore. We all swore."

"All?"

"The elders. The Council."

"Why?"

"For the good of Isis. That was Mark's argument. He had just been elected President when his father was killed in a rockslide. He was too young for the job. They should have picked one of the elders. But Mark was always ambitious. He swept aside all objections and got himself elected—the eldest of the Firsts. For the good of Isis was what he has always said. But I was never sure. All the crazy taboos about Guardian ... burying the past ... the way we treat the women ... just to hide... And now it has gone so far..." The old man's voice rumbled into silence.

"Gone where?" Jody prompted.

"Huh? What? Nowhere, Jody. Nothing."

Jody sighed impatiently. He dearly loved Grandfather, but his habit of drifting off into the past where you could not reach him was sometimes very trying. "Won't you at least tell me why the President seems to *expect* me to get into trouble—me more than anyone else. Sometimes I get the feeling that he's just waiting for me to make a mistake."

"Exactly." Grandfather pounded his fists feebly on the arms

of his chair. "Yet still you do these reckless things."

"I can't stop being myself and asking questions just because of a quarrel between ... well, between two *old men!*" He got the rudeness out in a rush and waited for the storm. It never came, and when he dared to look up the old man's eyes were twinkling, though his wrinkled face looked as stern as before.

"Why should it matter so much that it was *I* who broke a taboo?" he dared to go on. "If indeed I did. I asked Uncle Shaun if I could and he said not to touch because he said so, not because of any taboo."

"Such a self-important man," murmured Grandfather. "You were not told that the Gifts were taboo because they were not. There was no need. None of us who kept vigil in the Cave would ever have thought of touching any of them. But now they are taboo."

Jody took his time working this out. "Do you mean that the President changes the rules as he goes along? That's not fair."

"It is for the good of Isis," Grandfather quoted bitterly, his face twisting into even deeper wrinkles. "I must tell you just a little, so that you will understand. When I was a child I too broke a taboo, and nearly lost my life, besides risking ... the one who saved me."

"You did? What taboo? What happened?"

"Nothing. I was very small, and the idea of taboos was not fully understood. You see ..." Again he hesitated. "There were dangers we did not understand. To protect ourselves and especially the young children it was decided to have taboos. It was the very first one that I broke, not knowing what I was doing."

"Was it the Cave?"

"Oh, no. The Cave had not been made then."

"Not made? I don't understand. The *Guardian* made the Cave."

"So he did."

"But that was in the Beginning Time. Guardian made the sky and Ra and the stars and the whole of Isis and the Cave..."

"Nonsense. The Guardian made the Cave, certainly, but he didn't make Isis. Isis was already here."

"Are you sure?"

"Of course I am. As for the Cave, I saw him make that with

my own eyes."

"Honestly?"

"Oh, yes. That was something to behold. He held out his hand and a ray of red light like a rod shot out from his palm and where it struck the mesa the rocks melted away."

"Truly?"

"Yes, truly."

"What was he like, the Shining One?"

"Just the way you've heard in the stories. Tall and silvery-gold. He shone so that your eyes hurt and you had to turn away."

Jody nodded. That was how the Guardian of Isis would have to look. After a while he asked, "Did you see him again after that?"

"Never. When the Caves were made and the things put into them they left and never came back." There was an unexpected sadness in his voice. Jody looked up sharply.

"*They*?"

"Did I say they? I'm getting old. Don't pay attention. My tongue doesn't always say what my brain wishes it to. *He* left. Only he."

Jody went back to what they had been talking about before. "If you didn't break the taboo of the Cave, it must have been the taboo of the Mesa or the mountains, or the Wall or the Hobbit." He watched his grandfather's face. "Ah! It was the Wall, wasn't it? What did you do?"

"There was no Wall then."

"No *Wall*? Then you could see, with your own eyes ... see whatever ..."

"After what I did they built the Wall. It was my fault." Grandfather pressed his lips together.

"What is behind the Wall? Tell me."

"I cannot. I swore. We all swore."

"Grandfather, listen to me! The water in the lake is rising. Already it is washing over the stepping stones. If it goes on rising and doesn't stop it could fill the whole Valley. And I'm sure that whatever is behind the Wall has everything to do with why the water is rising."

"Fill our Valley? That cannot happen!"

"It might. Grandfather, I have been thinking. We always

61

take things for granted, as if they happened by magic. And we tell stories to explain the things we cannot understand. Like why Ra gets up in the same place every morning. But I don't believe in magic any more. I know the water comes down from the High Country where we may not go. It goes into the lake and from the lake it goes into Lost Creek. Then it vanishes under the archway in the Wall. Am I right?"

"Yes, yes. Of course you are right."

"Now, suddenly, the water is not going away. We cannot talk about it sensibly because of the taboo, but there are many stories to explain it. Some people say there is a great dragon in the Place of the Wall, some say it is the Hobbit itself; and it is very thirsty and it lies there all day and swallows up the river. Now if that is true, and the dragon or the Hobbit is no longer thirsty or has gone away, then what is going to happen to us? We will drown if the Valley fills with water, for we have nowhere else to go."

"Surely that will not happen."

"How can you be so sure? Unless you already know. The water rises a little more every day. Where does the water go unless there is Something behind the Wall to swallow it up." Craftily Jody watched the old man's hands, and saw them tighten on the arms of the chair. "There *is* Something behind the Wall that swallows up the river! Then why has it stopped and what are we to do? You must tell me, Grandfather."

"I cannot, Jody. I do not know. I was very young. It is like a bad dream. Please ask no more questions. The trouble will only become worse."

"All right, Grandfather. Be calm." Jody took a jug of summer-berry wine from the shelf and poured a glass for the old man. He sipped it gratefully and presently nodded.

"That is better. Pour one for yourself."

"Me?" The unmarried boys drank only at Thanksgiving.

"Why not? You are a man now. They have decided that." There was a bitterness in Grandfather's voice that made Jody stare; but the old man said nothing more. Jody poured himself a modest half-glassful of the sharp crimson wine and sat down again at Grandfather's feet.

"Now drink your wine and listen very carefully without asking questions all the time." Grandfather's voice was firm.

"You are in bad trouble. How bad may depend on how you answer the President when he questions you. This business about the water rising—that may be a useful distraction, only don't mention the Wall. You must say that while you were in the Cave there was much on your mind and that the Guardian spoke to you and told you how to make the new light happen."

"But it wasn't like that—at least not exactly ..." Jody stopped, confused. How had it been?

"Bother it, Jody. We're talking about your *life*. And how do you know that it wasn't the Guardian who put such a strange idea into your head? That magic wand has been in the Cave since before you were born, and nobody ever had the idea before that it would make the light come back. How do you know that it wasn't the Guardian?"

Jody's mind was in a fine muddle, not helped by the wine. What did Grandfather mean: We're talking about your life? He had just opened his mouth to ask when a noise outside the door made him quickly empty his glass and put it out of sight. He didn't want to get into more trouble.

The door swung open. Jody's father Isaac stood on the threshold. Behind him crowded his mother, softly weeping in her apron, his brothers, angry-faced, and the sisters-in-law, holding their children close.

"You are to come," Isaac said harshly. "The Council wishes to speak to you."

Jody tried to remember Grandfather's advice. Life was all such a muddle and had suddenly begun to move much too fast. He walked to the door, noticing how Mary and Debbie shrank back against the wall as he passed, pulling their children to them. Out of his way? Or so that he wouldn't touch them? He hardened his jaw and stuck his lower lip out. None of them should guess how he felt.

"Just one minute!"

They all turned. Grandfather was struggling out of his chair. "The Council is not complete yet. Isaac, give me your arm. Ingrid, where've you hidden my stick? So he thought he'd start without me, did he? Well, he's going to find that he's over-stepped the line this time, has Mark London!"

63

Chapter Six

For the first time in many years the Council of Seven sat in solemn conclave with all seven members. Jody was never to forget the moment when his grandfather hobbled across the threshold of the dining hall on the arm of his son, to take his rightful place at High Table on the Council of Isis.

Five of the men who were already assembled looked astonished and somewhat embarrassed at the sight of the old man. They were meek farmers, most of them, and for too long Mark London had been more than merely their leader. He had shaped both them and Isis into what he wanted them to be.

The old man pulled his crippled body upright when he reached the table. "I am here, Mark London, to see whether the meaning of justice and freedom has changed since the days when I last took part in this assembly."

The President had risen to his feet when he had seen his old enemy enter the room, and now he drew himself up to his full height, while his eyes flamed anger. For a while the others, sitting silently around the table, wondered if the brothers-in-law would come to blows, as they had done on two other memorable occasions—at the naming of the taboos, and at the marriage of the older Jody N'Kumo to the President's sister Carrie.

They looked at each other in silence. Then the President's eyes were hooded. He indicated the empty chair at the table with a wave of his hand. "You are welcome, brother."

Isaac helped his father into the chair, bowed politely to the assembly, and then swiftly left the room without even a glance at his son, who was left standing alone just inside the door.

"Come here, boy, and stand before us," the President's voice boomed.

"His name is Jody, Mark," reminded the older N'Kumo.

"What vanity made you name him after yourself?" snapped the President back.

"None of mine. It was the choice of my son."

"Nevertheless, it causes confusion. And the fact that he bears your name—the name of one of the Seven—may influence the others unfairly towards him."

"As it has influenced you in the past and even now? My dear Mark, after four generations most of the people on Isis share common ancestors. Surely none of us is the greater or the lesser because of our parentage?"

"But it is we, the surviving seven sons, who govern Isis. The power is in *our* hands. And he is *your* grandson."

"The power *is* in our hands." Jody's grandfather repeated the phrase softly. "Let us use it gently and with wisdom, not in anger, my dear Mark."

Grandfather N'Kumo sat back in his chair, easing his twisted spine against the unyielding wood. The other five stirred and rustled, looking at each other sideways, carefully. The President took the central chair and stared coldly at Jody. Jody stood straight, his hands tight by his sides. He felt his jaw wobble, and he clenched it and stuck out his lower lip defiantly. The President's eyes burned into his, but he would not let his gaze falter.

Into the tense silence crept a little tune. Grandfather was humming under his breath, as if unaware of what he was doing, one of the ditties that the small ones sang as they played their game of catch. One of the others nudged him and he looked up and stopped. But the spell was broken. Jody saw the anger flare in the President's face. He pushed back his chair with an ugly rasp against the flagstone floor and shouted the one word: "Sacrilege!" hitting the table with the flat of his hand to emphasise the word.

"That has still to be proved, Mark." The mild voice of Grandfather N'Kumo broke the silence.

"The boy's actions speak for themselves."

"Actions may be interpreted in different ways. And surely his intent must carry some weight."

"Intent?"

"Have you asked Jody why he did what he did?"

"Why should I? His behaviour is all of a piece. He has always been rebellious, always. He questions our ways, the old ways, the tried ways. When he should be out hunting with the younger Thirds or with the Fourths he is off by himself, his mind wandering along dangerous paths. I have seen the things he has made."

65

"He is young, Mark. They are only toys. A child's toys."

"I am not a fool, Jody N'Kumo, nor one of the kitchen aunties. The boy is not a child and those are not toys that occupy his time. They are inventions. Tools of the devil. His ways are not our ways and he will not conform. What he did in the Cave was all of a piece with the way in which he has always run counter to my—to *our* decisions and orders."

"Nevertheless, Mark, you must let Jody speak."

"*Must?*" The President's head poked forward. But there was a mutter of approval from the other five, who had sat silent during this exchange. Perhaps the President realised that he was losing control. He might rage inwardly at the power his old enemy still seemed to hold, crippled and helpless though he might be, but he was careful not to let them see how it disturbed him. He spread his hands in a gesture of submission, and forced a cold smile onto the rock of his face.

"So, let the boy speak."

"Jody." Grandfather beckoned him close. As he looked down Jody could see the warning in the old man's brown eyes. "Tell the Council exactly how it came about that you touched one of the Gifts of the Guardian."

Jody swallowed and faced the Council. Instinctively he knew that to address himself to the President was useless. His mind was already made up, and not all the words on Isis would change it. So it was to the silent five that he spoke, willing them to understand and to side with Grandfather when it came to the vote.

"The water in the lake is rising," he began abruptly, remembering what Grandfather had told him. "Every time I looked it was higher. It was to look at it again that I rose early on the morning after Thanksgiving, and so was led by the Guardian to find his Gift."

He wetted his lips. So far so good. Out of the corner of his eye he thought he could see a gleam of approval in Grandfather's eyes.

"I could not believe that such a thing was happening to me," he went on. "That *I* should keep vigil in the Cave. I suppose everyone else was as surprised, and nobody thought to provide me with a fresh candle. After a while it began to grow dim and I thought—suppose I cannot find my way out when it is dark?

Suppose I knock against the table and damage one of the gifts because I cannot see? At that moment my eye fell on the sacred white wand, and into my mind flashed the idea that it was the same as the wand in the ceiling, from which the light used to come before the Guardian took it away."

Unconsciously Jody's voice had fallen into the singsong of the story-tellers of Isis. The five were watching him now, listening to every word. It was going to be all right, he thought, and finished his story. "So I exchanged the two wands, and put the new magic in the place of that which was worn out, and behold, the Cave was filled with light and I could see!"

The five stirred, looking at each other, nodding. Angus McCann, who was next in age to the President, moved his hands as though silently clapping. The President frowned and the five subsided into stillness again. Jody had not won yet.

He no longer knew what to say. What else *could* he say? A sidelong glance at Grandfather told him nothing. The old man's face might have been carved out of black stone for all the expression it held. Why doesn't he help me, give me a hint? thought Jody frantically. Then he saw that the President too was watching Grandfather—watching him the way the cliff-eagles watch the movement of rock-bunnies on the scree below the mesa, soaring, almost motionless, waiting for the tiny involuntary movement below. Then the sudden swoop, the inevitable kill.

Jody did not look at Grandfather again. He stood facing the table and did the hardest thing he had to do in his whole life. He said nothing.

In the silence he could feel the President's anger grow. And he knew that he was winning. The President was angry because Jody had not trapped himself in such a way that it would be easy to punish him. Now I understand how his mind works, thought Jody gleefully, and a small spark of pride caught fire inside him. When Angus McCann questioned him he answered readily.

"The water? Yes, I could see it rise. I began to think that if there was a way to measure it, day by day, I could tell if it was continuing to rise or if it was beginning to go down again."

"And have you thought of such a way?" McCann's voice was kind and full of interest.

It had been a long time since anyone had been interested in his ideas. "A stick perhaps." Jody spoke enthusiastically as the idea

67

took shape in his mind again. "With markings every thumb joint or so, so that we could see just how far the water had risen. Like on..." He stopped, suddenly aware of danger.

The President's voice was very soft. He was like a spider, slowly and carefully weaving his web. "Like the last Gift of the Guardian? Is that what you believe the Guardian gave us that Gift for? Did you think of that by yourself, or did the Guardian put *that* idea in your mind also?"

"I..." Jody did not know how to answer. This was like a game, only he did not know the rules. "The idea came. That's all. But it's right. I just know it is." Enthusiasm overcame caution and he went on in a rush. "That *must* be what the Gift is for. The spike has to go in the ground, you see, at the old shore line. Then the marks will tell us how far the water has risen each day. But why does the colour change from black to red?" He was talking to himself now, frowning over the problem. He did not look at Grandfather. He did not see the almost imperceptible shake of the old man's head. His mind was entirely filled with the excitement of the giant step into a new way of thinking.

"When the water reaches the red mark it must mean something very important. Red is an important colour. The cloth on the stick was red. Perhaps the water will go down then... but if that is so why should the stick be necessary? No, it must mean that if the water rises *that* high, then it will go on rising until the whole of our Valley is flooded. Unless we do something about it."

The five stirred anxiously. The other two members of the Council did not move. Grandfather was hunched over in his chair, looking down at the swollen hands twisted together in his lap. The President sat erect, very still, lightly holding the threads of his web. His eyes gleamed. He pounced.

"Are you telling us that you cannot say precisely what the Guardian means by his Gift? You are not wholly in his mind? I am surprised, boy. I had thought that you and the Guardian were as one."

Jody's head jerked up. His skin tightened with shock. "No, sir. That would be sacrilege," he gasped.

"Yes. That would indeed be sacrilege. But let us suppose just for now that you *are* in the Guardian's mind, or he in yours. Let us suppose that the water does rise above the red mark on the sacred stick. What would you have us do then?"

"I?"

"My pardon. What would the *Guardian* have us do?"

The threads began to tighten. "I don't know. What choice is there? If the Valley was flooded we would either have to leave, which is impossible, or force the water to go back where it belongs."

"Which is . . ?"

"I don't know. How should I know?" Jody wailed, struggling like a fly in the web. The President's eyes were like points of fire. They fastened themselves on Jody's face, and Jody found that he could not turn away. He had often despised the five for the weak way in which they had allowed the President to lead them wherever he wished. Now he had a taste of the President's powers himself.

"The river goes into the Place of the Wall," he said reluctantly at last. "We all know that. And it does not come out again. Whatever has happened has happened within the Place, and it is there that it must be put right." Why had he said that? He had not meant to. It was as if the words had been dragged out of him . . .

There was the sound of a faint sigh in the silent room. It did not come from the President, but from Grandfather N'Kumo. The President's hands relaxed. For the first time he looked directly at the other members of the Council. There was nothing forced about his smile now.

"Something must be put right within the Place of the Wall," he repeated softly. "You heard the boy. Our ways have been changed. Our sacred taboos have been ignored. Now the water is rising. But all is not lost. We have been given a sign. Nothing could be clearer than that."

"Poppycock!" said Grandfather, very loudly.

The five gasped. Even Jody was shocked. But it appeared that the President was not upset. The President was enjoying himself. "So history repeats itself," he said softly, and it was clear from the expressions on the other faces that the six Councillors knew what he meant.

"Has he committed sacrilege, or has he not?" the President went on. "It comes to my mind that we can very easily test this boy. I remember stories of how witches were tested in the long-

69

ago times. We can test this boy in like manner. No... Listen first." His hand lifted as a murmur ran around the table. It died away and he went on. "I too have been aware of the rising water, and I have been waiting for a sign. We have it here in the boy. If there is danger to the people of Isis we must find out exactly what the danger is, and what we can do about it. We look to the Guardian for protection, and yet it is many years since the voice of the Shining One was heard from within the Sacred Cave. Has he abandoned us? No, because he has sent us a Gift in our hour of need. But why do we no longer hear him? Perhaps it is because he is waiting for one of *us* to come to *him*!"

A gasp ran around the table. Grandfather N'Kumo bent his forehead towards his clasped hands.

"But who can we send on this perilous journey?" the President went on, smiling amiably at the stunned faces around the table. "Who can we choose? Why, who but the one whom the Guardian has already singled out for his special favour!"

"You devil! No!" Grandfather N'Kumo's voice seemed wrung out of the depths of his being.

"No? You mean that you do not believe that your grandson was chosen by the Guardian? In spite of his 'luck' in the hunt? In spite of being drawn to be a Bearer, and that in the most dangerous position? In spite of being chosen to find the Gift? In spite of being the agent through whom the Guardian has restored light to the Sacred Cave? And you still do not believe he is chosen? But if you do not believe that, then you must know that the boy has committed sacrilege in meddling with the Gifts. And the penalty for sacrilege is death!"

"For God's sake, Mark. Not since our coming to Isis has a man taken another man's life. Let us not begin now." It was Angus McCann who spoke, and there was a general mutter of agreement.

Grandfather did not speak, but he raised his bowed head and looked at the President; the President stared arrogantly down at the crippled old man. Their eyes battled each other. They were like two men playing at long-sticks, thought Jody. But the game was too unevenly matched. It wasn't fair. The President was tall, gaunt, strong as whipcord, completely in command. Grandfather was bent and sick, hurting with a pain, Jody realised, that had come about because of what *he* had done. He

70

wanted to go down on his knees beside the old man and beg his pardon, and promise never to invent anything again, never to day-dream, never to question the ways of the people. Only it was too late. The damage had already been done.

"Do not be concerned, brother Angus," the President declared solemnly. "I promise you that no man's hand shall be raised against this boy, since after all it is quite possible that he *is* the Guardian's chosen one."

Jody's heart gave a sudden thankful lurch. A smile began to tug at the corners of his mouth. But the President's next words wiped it from his face.

"We will send him as our emissary into the land of the Guardian, to ask the help of the Shining One in saving our Valley from the flood. If he is indeed under his protection, then no harm will come to him. If, on the other hand..." He raised his hands and then let them fall to the table. "The Guardian alone knows for sure whether the boy has committed sacrilege or not. So let his fate be in the Guardian's hands."

"You are sending my grandson to his death, Mark London, and you know it," whispered Grandfather N'Kumo.

"To his death? Do *you* not believe that the Guardian will protect him if he has done no wrong, even as he saved me from falling from the mesa?" He turned quickly to the five without waiting for the old man's answer. "What do *you* say?"

One by one they gave their assent, reluctantly, but they gave it. Send him... He must go... To the Guardian... Let the Guardian decide... Yes, let the Shining One decide.

With a groan Grandfather N'Kumo struggled to his feet. "You are twisting the truth, Mark, as you have always twisted it. The others have forgotten how things really were back then. But *I* have not forgotten. I remember the Keeper of the Light. I do not fear That Old Woman as you..."

"Silence! Now. At once. Or by Ra you will go with your grandson!"

"I wish I could," the old man whispered. "To see that face that you have mocked and lied about... Come, Jody, help me out of here. I will not take my place in this assembly again." He turned his back on the six men who had been his boyhood friends in the long ago days when they and Isis had been young together. The tears made shining furrows down his black cheeks. His head shook.

"Tomorrow morning," the President shouted in a sudden passion, at what Jody could not understand. After all, he had won, had he not? "Tomorrow, when Ra is cut in half by the eastern peak, you will leave the Valley. Is that clear?"

Jody's head went up proudly. If he was to go to his death, and surely that must be so, then he would go as a N'Kumo, not like some criminal begging for mercy. "I shall be ready," he said clearly.

Chapter Seven

Jody lay on his back and stared up at the dark ceiling. The family had left him, and at last he was alone, but still he could not sleep. The evening had been hard to bear. When he had been ordered to appear before the Council his family had drawn away from him as if he had some horrible disease—even his own brothers.

But once the verdict was announced they were all over him, patting him, hugging him. His mother and sisters-in-law fussed over food and clothes for the journey, and his father and brothers argued about which weapons he should take.

Jody took no part in the discussion. He looked at his grandfather, silent, motionless in his chair; and he reached out to the old man across their silence. The chattering of the others, their fussing and even their affection, seemed artificial and forced. It was as if he were already dead and they were preparing him for the journey to That Old Woman. Only in the silence between him and Grandfather could he find any truth.

It was late before all the preparations were completed, and one by one the family slipped away to their own rooms. His mother patted his shoulder. "Sleep now. You need the rest. It will be a long day tomorrow." She choked on the words and went out of the room quickly, leaving Jody and his father alone.

They looked at each other warily. Isaac had never had much to say to his son. Jody fitted into none of the patterns that his father could understand. At this moment Isaac was profoundly uncomfortable. He looked at the floor, shuffling his feet in the house-slippers one of his daughters-in-law had knitted for him.

"Yes. Well. I think we have got together everything you will need. Goodnight, son." He left the room quickly. Jody longed to be able to reach out and hug the inarticulate farmer who was his beginning; but the shell around the older man was too thick to break through and the years of misunderstanding lay too heavy between them.

"Goodnight, Father. Sleep well," he answered automatically. The door shut and he was alone. Since his brothers had married and this room had been his alone he had enjoyed being able to close the door against the rest of the too close, neighbourly, gossiping, eyes-everywhere community. But on this night the loneliness began to press in on him. There was nothing to get between him and his thoughts, and he didn't want to think. Not now.

Why did he have to be different from everyone else? He hadn't asked to be that way. All the others seemed to work together in harmony. All the others were contented with their life exactly as it was. It seemed that only he was quarrelsome and contentious. Only *he* thought the kind of thoughts and asked the kind of questions that could not be answered, that set the others at odds with him.

If Jody had only had a close friend to confide in, he might have been surprised to find that there was plenty of quarrelling and contention in the community, from the historic enmity between the President and Jody's grandfather, down to the small angers between siblings as to who should get the last piece of wild honeycomb from the communal dish.

But Jody had always been a loner. As he lay in his bed in the long dark he began to see himself as more and more different, more and more separate. Slowly the idea grew in his mind that the sentence of the Council had been a just one. For the sake of the wholeness of the community he must go. It was a heavy sorrow, and the greatest burden he had ever had to shoulder, but he accepted it.

Not for an instant did Jody believe the story that he was being sent as an emissary to the Guardian. That was a polite fiction to cover up the unmentionable: that in expelling him from the Valley and sending him north, the people of Isis were sending him to That Old Woman, the Ugly One, who waits on the other side of every man's last sleep. He knew, as the Council had known, that there was no life for people on Upper Isis, where the lips turned blue and a weight on the chest set a man gasping painfully for air. Up there on the heights Ra's fire burned the skin, and there were strange sicknesses from which there was no recovery.

Jody looked squarely at these facts; and after a time the fear that had fluttered inside his chest like a netted bird was quieted. He felt very sad at leaving his family and the interesting world that he had known for such a short time, but with the sadness came calmness and strength.

He sat up in bed and struck a flint to light his candle. Piled against the wall he could see the mound of provisions, weapons and clothes that his family had collected for his going. It would take four strong men to carry them all. He picked out a thick blanket, a good knife made of the old metal from the Beginning Times, fishing tackle, his own familiar sling, a spare pair of sandals, a water flask, two flat loaves of bread and a small round cheese. He made a neat bundle of all this, tied it securely with a length of good grass rope, and then, still wrapped in the same quiet calm, he lay down and went instantly to sleep.

He woke, just as he had intended, in the pearly pre-dawn light. It took him only a moment to slip on his shirt and breeches, to strap his bare feet into sandals, and to pick up his bundle and loop it over his shoulders in such a way that both arms would be free. Then he eased open the door and padded softly down the passage and out of the family house.

He did not look back. He plodded quietly up the river bank to where the sound of the Cascades boomed loudly in his ears, the only sound in the pre-dawn hush. Only once, at the foot of the waterfall, he allowed himself one quick backward glance, at the village where he had been born, at the lake and the wide grass-filled Valley that was the whole small world of his people.

Even with his bundle across his back the climb was not nearly as difficult this time. He knew it could be done and that was half the battle. It was not long before he was at the top, staring north, while the steady wind dried his clothes, and his gasping subsided to manageable breaths again. The air was thin up here, but he *could* breathe it. He would walk slowly, he decided, and rest whenever he was tired. After all, there was no hurry. He was not going anywhere in particular. He would keep as much as possible to the low parts of the country, and follow the river to its source. After that he did not know.

If he could hunt he would be able to cook and eat whatever he caught. If there was no game he would eat bread and cheese. As long as he walked close to the river, water would be no problem. When the food was gone, or when he was too tired to walk, or if the sickness of Ra came on him, then he would rest and wait for the Ugly One to come and find him. It was all very simple and straightforward.

Ahead of him great mountains tumbled away to left and right in billows of red and purple rock. Between them wound the silver thread of the river. It twisted to left and right between sloping flanks of tussocky blue-grass and silver thorn bushes. He could see only glimpses of it, here and there. But he knew it was there and he knew that with all its twistings and turnings it travelled north, away from the Valley. That was the way he must go to meet his fate. Whether it would be the Shining One or That Old Woman whom he would meet was out of his hands.

He had no way of knowing how far he walked that first day, or any of the other days that followed. Where the steep flanks of mountains crowded close, he walked along the river bank over stones and piles of shale and the going was slow and painful. Where the mountains drew back and gave the river room to meander, he walked across upland meadows until the mountains began to crowd together again.

It was pleasant walking through the knee-high grass and the sharp-scented flowering herbs that grew among it. Jody marked with his eye where the valley narrowed and the river seemed to vanish into the mountains, and then walked steadily towards that spot without having to be concerned as to where he placed each footstep.

Where the mountains crowded in the walking was tiring and often dangerous. He found it was safer to slip off his sandals and cling bare-toed to rocks that were slippery with spray from the fast river. Sometimes the walls rose sheer above him on either side, and the river had no banks at all. Then he had to wade waist-high, pushing the icy water away with each staggering step forward.

Once, at the bottom of a rocky gorge, the light of Ra was hidden and midday turned suddenly into a chill twilight. That was the worst place, the place where he nearly gave up. But he didn't. Some obstinacy inside him made him struggle on until, as suddenly, the sides of the gorge fell away, Ra's heat once more comforted his frozen body, and he was able to scramble out of the river onto the verge and rest and get warm again.

The first day he didn't feel like hunting. He ate a morsel of bread at noon, and when twilight found him at the neck of a wide grassy valley, he climbed thankfully away from the water, and staggered on numb legs to where a rocky western slope still held some of Ra's heat. He made himself gather sticks and grass—as in his own valley, there was little useful firewood—and build a fire at which to dry his clothes. He rolled himself naked in his blanket while they dried, spread out on the rocks. Then he ate some bread and cheese, drank a little water and lay down to sleep.

He was cold, and sleep was hard to find. His thoughts kept drifting back to the Village. He found himself seeing his mother's face, his brothers'. He wondered what they must have thought when they went to wake him that morning and found him already gone. Each time his thoughts returned to the Village he resolutely switched them away. There *was* no past for him. There was only the *now* of this last journey north.

He slept at last and woke to feel Ra's rays baking his skin. His nose and forehead itched with yesterday's sunburn, and he wished he had thought to bring some kind of head-covering. Ra's heat was indeed much fiercer on the high ground, away from his Valley.

When he stood up to put his clothes on he felt dizzy and light-headed and very hungry. He went down to the river to wash and drink, and, among the speckled stones, saw the freckled shapes of pinkies. He went back for his line, tied on a hook and baited it with a beetle, still wriggling its shiny dark legs as he dropped it into the water. Before he had time to get any hungrier he had caught two fat fish. He quickly made a fire and laid the fish on flat stones close to the heat, while he fed the tiny fire with dry thorn sticks, which burned with a fierce heat, but so quickly that feeding the fire had to be a continuous process.

He ate the fish in his fingers off the hot stones, while the fire's embers wriggled into grey ash. The flesh was pink and sweet, subtly flavoured with the spicy aroma of thorn bush smoke. He ate with concentration until there was not a shred of flesh left. Alone in this strange valley, only an arm's length away from death, the food was tastier than any meal he could remember in his whole life before. When he had finished he licked his fingers carefully, scraped a hole in the sandy soil to bury the bones and heads of the pinkies, and then went back to the river to wash and drink.

The Valley was long rather than wide, and Jody reckoned that it would take almost half a day to traverse its length. He decided to wait until the most scorching part of the day was past before setting out. He found a shadow cast by a big rock and lay there, warm, peaceful, full-stomached, his head on his bundle, until, when Ra was well over his left shoulder, he set out again.

It was a very strange journey. Up until this time, all of Isis had been the wide dish-like Valley of head-high red-grass, the slopes of short blue-grass and red scree, the towering mesa and the impassable mountains that rimmed his world. It would not have been a great surprise to have found beyond those encircling mountains nothing but the emptiness of starlit space, as the Fourths believed, or a world full of mists or storms, or inhabited by nightmare creatures. Where nothing was known, anything was possible.

Every day as Jody walked steadily northward he expected the unexpected. Each time he pushed through a river-hewn gorge between crowding mountains, he thought that now, at last, he must have come to World's End. Each time it was the lack of anything surprising that was the surprise. Nothing seemed to change as he slowly followed the river upward to its source.

In fact something *was* changing, but it was happening so slowly that Jody was not consciously aware of it. If he had stopped to think that water always runs downhill, and that he had been walking upstream for day after day, he would have realised that he was climbing slowly but steadily towards Upper Isis. The slope was too gradual for him to be aware of it, though after five days the thin air began to make him light-headed. His chest hurt him all the time. It was a dull nagging pain that he accepted unquestioningly as part of his new life, like the blisters on his feet, the sunburn, and the unexpected fits of drowsiness that sometimes overcame him even at noon.

He lost count of days. He even began to forget about his Valley. His life narrowed down to a sleep under the stars, wakening to Ra shining on his face, fishing for breakfast, eating early-ripening summer-berries for lunch, and hunting for rock-bunnies or fishing again for his supper. In between these events he walked. And rested. And walked again. And fell asleep, tired out, panting for air, under the stars.

He had stopped thinking about the Guardian. If the Shining

One had not shown himself by now, it was surely because he did not wish to be seen. As for That Old Woman, he thought about her only in moments of unexpected terror, such as the time when his foot slipped sideways on a treacherously slippery rock and he nearly pitched head first into a foaming whirlpool. His heart had pounded and the sweat had broken out on his forehead as he realised how close he had been to death. But he had recovered himself and scrambled to safety, and after a little while the monotony of his walking blotted out the face of the Ugly One and he forgot how close she had been to him in that moment.

After many days the river became narrower, more swift, more urgent. Jody became aware that he was climbing, constantly, up one set of shallow waterfalls after another, that led like silver steps up to a high col between two great mountains. He stared up at the dizzy heights through sweat-bleared eyes, and knew that he had come to a choice.

He must either risk the climb to the top, which was higher than a man could possibly go, and get down quickly into the more breathable air on the other side, if, indeed, there was a valley on the other side; or he must stay where he was and wait for That Old Woman to come to him.

There was just enough of the old Jody left to stick out his lower lip and set his teeth together in a grin that had no humour in it. He slept where he was, close to the falls, with the sound of the water pounding in his ears; and in the morning he set his hands and feet to the slippery rock and began to climb.

He moved very slowly. An eagle, sailing on a column of warm air above the valley behind him, would hardly have been able to detect any movement from the tiny figure. Yet it seemed to Jody that he was climbing at full tilt; only that, oddly, as he climbed it seemed that the rocks stretched away above him, becoming taller and taller the faster he climbed.

After a time he forgot where he was and began to think that he was climbing the Cascades at the head of his own Valley. He thought that he was at the very beginning of his journey, and he wondered vaguely why he should be so tired after a good night's sleep in his own bed. But, slowly, laboriously, one foot after another, broken fingernails clawing for handholds, he climbed on.

Then there came a moment when he pulled himself up, and in front of him there was no more vertical rock, but a gentle slope of turf. At first he did not know what to do. His body had become a climbing machine, and his mind had stopped thinking a long time ago. He crawled forward across the unaccustomed softness, and lay sprawled with his face in the grass. His eyes closed. His heart pounded like an animal trying to get out of a trap. He could feel it clawing inside his chest.

A long time later he pushed himself up and looked about him. The river, *his* river, that he had followed, it seemed, half across Isis, dwindled away upon the mountainside to his left in a thread of silver, falling, falling, from unbelievable heights. To his right was another mountain, almost as high. Ahead of him the gentle slope led upward to a gap between the two, and beyond that he could see nothing but sky.

On hands and knees he pulled himself up the slope, groaning at the effort, until he reached the highest point and could at last look down into the world that lay beyond the river's end. He expected that now, at last, he had come to the End of the World. He had no idea what it would look like. Would it be as black as night and full of stars? Would it be as blue as a skyful of noon? Or, since the storms that swept across Isis had to come from the north somewhere, would he see a howling vortex of red sand? Nothing would have surprised him.

Nothing except what he saw. For the last thing he expected was a gentle valley, sloping down from the heights in a series of misty terraces of red, soft blue and silver. From the far sides of the mountains to either side of him silver streams twisted, spread and came together to form a new river, a river that flowed from just below the ledge where he lay, in a series of falls that shimmered in misty colours and then looped lazily across the long valley until it became too small to be seen, and was swallowed up in a rim of hills so far away and blurred by mist that at first he had mistaken them for a low line of clouds.

Jody lay in pain and yet in peace. Was this the valley where one went after death? Had That Old Woman touched him, and he had not even seen her nor been aware of her presence? But his fingers still bled, and each breath he drew sent stabbing knives into his sides, so perhaps he was still alive.

Alive or dead, this beauteous valley was where he wished to

be. Slipping, sliding, rolling, he went down the turfy slope beside the river and the waterfalls. It had taken him from Ra-up almost to Ra-down to climb the rocky stairway to the watershed. He fell down its northern slope in the space of a few heart-beats. He rolled. Staggered to his feet. Fell and rolled again, until at length he came to rest in an upland meadow of blue-grass, in the shadow of a grove of enormous bamboo, bigger than any he had ever seen.

He lay where he had fallen. After a time the tearing pain in his chest became a little more bearable, and the noise of his gasping and the thumping agony of his heart lessened. He rolled over on his back and found that he was looking up into the sky through the silver tatters of bamboo leaves. Far, far above his head the wind stirred the tips of the canes, and as they knocked against each other they made a soft booming music, deep and noble. Jody lay and listened to the music and after a while his eyes closed and he slept.

He did not sleep for long. Ra was still sending long mountain shadows across the valley when he was wakened with shocking suddenness by a high yammering cry that made the hair on the back of his neck bristle and sent a shiver right down his spine. He jerked his sore body to its knees and stared dizzily around. Nothing stirred in the gentle valley except the bamboos, and there was no sound except the soft deep boom-boom of their stems.

He ran a hand through his hair and licked his dry cracked lips. Had he dreamed that fearsome noise? He struggled to his feet with a groan and looked around for the bundle which he had brought so far and which had somehow parted company with him on the last wild tumble down into the valley. Something flashed in the corner of his eye, and with a hunter's instinct he fumbled a stone into his sling and raised his arm.

It streaked down from the mountain to his right. Now it was at the place where he had crossed the watershed. Now it was bounding down the precipitous slope of turf and scree and thorn bush. Now it was close enough to see in its immensity and the horror of its total strangeness.

There must be no other creature like it on Isis. It was a four-legged beast, twice as long as a full-grown man is tall, with a tail as long again, that feathered out behind it as it ran. There were sharp spines rising from its bony back, like nothing Jody had ever seen on an animal before, and its great claws struck sparks from the stones as it bounded towards him. It was close enough now for Jody to be able to see the wide mouth, dripping saliva, the long tongue hanging out between teeth as sharp as arrow-tips.

Jody steadied his feet and sent the sling swinging in a wide arc so that it hissed softly through the air. By now he could see the monster's eyes, fiery red and wickedly slanting, and he made ready to give the little jerk that would send the stone spinning from the sling, straight for the monster's head.

'NO!' A great voice cried out from behind him. It was too late to stop the motion of his arm and hand. All he could do was to move as the stone was loosed, so that it shot harmlessly by the creature's left ear. Its forward rush did not hesitate, and Jody waited, bracing himself against the onslaught of teeth and claws. Less than an arm's span away the creature rushed harmlessly by him. He felt the hairs on its flailing tail whip the skin of his bare arm as it passed.

Jody turned slowly. Coming through the shadowy grove towards him was a being shaped like a man, walking like a man, but enormously tall, taller by more than a head than Lars Petersen, who was the tallest man on Isis. His whole being seemed to glow with a silver-gold light so strong that Jody's hand went instinctively up to shade his eyes. He could not see if the being was naked or if he wore clothes like the people of Isis. The glow from his body seemed to cast a halo of light around him which blotted out detail. It was like trying to look for mountains on Ra itself. The light was too strong, too overwhelming.

Jody let his sling fall to the ground, and he himself fell on his face before the being, his arms stretched out before him. A deep thankfulness and amazement filled him. He had come into this strange country with no idea of where he was to go, except that it was probably to meet his death. But instead of That Old Woman he had met, as casually as one might meet a friend on a stroll, the Guardian of all Isis, the Shining One himself.

Chapter Eight

The wiry grass prickled Jody's face. He lay still, his heart thumping so suffocatingly that he did not at first hear the words that were spoken to him. They were repeated. The voice was clear and cool, each word separated from its neighbour, not run together the way ordinary people talked. It was a God-voice, Jody thought, not one of flesh and blood.

"Why are you lying on the ground, boy?" the voice asked. "Are you injured?"

"Sir?" Jody raised his head. "Lord?" What did one call the Guardian of all Isis? Blinded by the silver-gold light he shut his eyes. Perhaps even to look was taboo. "Do you wish me rather to kneel, Lord?" he asked humbly.

There was a pause. Then, "To *me*? Certainly not!"

Jody scrambled to his feet and stood awkwardly, his eyes lowered, his whole body tinglingly aware of the presence of the Great and Shining One. He was filled with joy and a breathless awe; and whatever was asked of him, no matter how impossible it might seem, he swore to himself that he would do it.

The command was surprising. "You had better come over here and make friends with Hobbit. Don't be afraid. His looks are deceiving. He is very friendly, though quite old."

"*This* is Hobbit?" He walked a few reluctant steps forward, steeling himself to meet the monster's teeth.

"You have heard of Hobbit?"

"Yes, indeed, Lord. Though I have never seen him. But in the stories of the Beginning Time it is said that once, long ago, one of our people killed a monster called Hobbit, and because of it the Light went out of the Valley and the curse of That Old Woman came upon our people. From that time Hobbit has been taboo. But we have never seen such a creature and we thought that perhaps there was only the one."

Only after Jody had rattled off the familiar tale did the meaning of the words sink in. He gasped and fell to his knees. "This is that one? Oh, forgive me for raising my hand to you, monster Hobbit. I did not know you. Kill me now, please, and do not let the curse fall on the rest ot my people."

An armlong length of rough wet tongue swept out and licked his face in one soaking swipe from throat to forehead. Jody fell back on his heels, his eyes wide open in surprise. Hobbit, obviously recognising a game when he saw one, sprang forward and planted his front paws on Jody's shoulders. It grinned.

Now that the creature was only a breath's distance away Jody could see that the red eyes which had seemed to slant so wickedly were really kind; and the dreadful teeth and the barbed back, which had sent shivers of fear down his spine, were but the creature's natural armour. He collapsed on his back, the creature striding him, and laughed, half with relief that the Ugly One was not going to take him to her kingdom, and half to hide the fact that he was still rather afraid of a creature so enormous and overpowering.

"Off, Hobbit!" the Shining One commanded, and instantly the creature sprang back, releasing Jody. It leapt with an odd bounding motion around the two, and then, just as suddenly, streaked off uphill, its reddish brown coat soon to be lost among the red and purple rocks.

"He was fun," said Jody, with only a small quaver in his voice. He still did not look up at the Shining One, and so did not see him begin to speak, then smile and shrug. Jody stood politely, staring at the ground, waiting for something to happen. In this land he was the stranger.

The other looked at him for a while and seemed to meditate. Then he asked in a mild voice, "Who are you? Why have you come?"

Jody bowed until his forehead touched his knees. "Lord, I am Jody N'Kumo, son of Isaac, grandson of Jody. I was sent here by the people of Isis to find you and ask for your help."

"You travelled here like that?" An unbearably bright hand gestured at Jody's tattered shirt and breeches, his sandals worn out, their straps mended and remended, his blanket roll battered and dusty from the sudden descent from the heights. "Where is your breather? Where is your UVO suit?" The voice was stern.

Jody's heart thumped. "Lord, I do not understand those things, but I regret if ... if I am improperly dressed to appear before you."

"It is your safety that concerns me, not how you appear. To travel with no suit or breather ... Why would your people put you in such danger when they could have called me over the radio and I would have come?"

"I am very sorry, Lord. I do not know that word—radio—either. As for danger, I think the President would have been most pleased if That Old Woman had found me before you did. The others too. I only made trouble."

"That Old Woman?"

"You know, Lord." Jody's voice fell to a whisper. "The Ugly One. She who lives in the far north and brings darkness and death to all people in the end. I thought perhaps the Hobbit was She, until you called its name."

"And what name do your people give to That Old Woman?"

"Lord, you must know that she is nameless."

The Guardian shook his head. "This has gone beyond my kind of understanding," he said surprisingly. "I must take you to talk with one who is wiser than I."

"There is another like you?"

"Not like me, no. She is wise, whereas I am only clever. She is my mistress."

"You are the *Guardian*. How can anyone be above you?"

"You will see."

Jody drew back.

"Does she have a name?" he asked, dry-lipped. "This mistress of yours?"

There was amusement in the precise voice that answered him. "Oh, yes. She is not nameless, Jody N'Kumo. There is no need for fear. Her name is Olwen."

So Jody willingly followed the Shining One through the tall stems of the bamboos. Ra set behind the western mountains in a glow of pale gold, and the long spring twilight began. A strange thing happened. Jody found that he could now look directly at the Shining One without his eyes watering. The details were no longer blurred, and he could see that the Guardian was very smooth, with a smoothness that seemed to belong to the Beginning Times. When he turned to make sure that Jody was following him, Jody could see that his eyes were like precious crystals, and that there was no hair anywhere on his face or head, but that it was as naked as a huge shining egg.

The Guardian walked slowly down the slope of the grove, but his stride was so long that Jody had almost to run to keep up with him. The bamboo stems cast long shadows along the ground, and the stems themselves seemed to be made half of shadow and half of the glowing light reflected out of the western sky. The whole grove seemed to be criss-crossed with alternate bands of black and gold until Jody's head was spinning and he could no longer distinguish the reality from the shadow. He staggered repeatedly and fell against the stems, and they responded with a hollow bong-bong, as, far above, their tips stirred and knocked against each other.

Beyond the grove the ground dropped gradually away to the river, which fell in a series of gentle waterfalls, like wide silver steps, to a still pool, before threading its lazy way across the plain to the far horizon. Jody's head spun.

As they left the grove the Guardian turned to him. "I will carry you now. Do not be afraid. It is a hard climb, and I must move rapidly, for you do not have enough space in your small lungs to breathe at the heights to which we must go."

He gave Jody no time to protest, but picked him up as casually as if he were a sack of grain, and draped him over his left shoulder, so that for the rest of that strange journey Jody saw everything upside down. The Guardian's stride lengthened, and Jody realised that up until then he had been accommodating it to Jody's shorter legs. They fairly sped over the ground, and when they began to climb in earnest it seemed to make no difference at all. Where a human would have gasped and hesitated or paused to rest, the Shining One climbed on with a smooth effortlessness.

Does a god have a heartbeat? Jody wondered. As his head bumped against the back of the Guardian he thought he heard the faintest of sounds, like the hum of a bee searching for honey. Faint and steady. Unchanging.

Even though he was making no effort, but just lay inertly over the shoulder of the Shining One, Jody began to feel as if he had been running. His chest hurt more than it had ever done before, and his head swam dizzily. They must be climbing very high indeed. He shut his eyes at the thought. What would become of him on the heights? Did not the Guardian know that they were taboo to the people? But surely the Guardian knew everything.

As if he could read his mind, the Guardian suddenly spoke. "Be still, Jody. It will not be long now. Soon we will help you to breathe comfortably." The words buzzed inside his head. They were the last sounds Jody heard as the darkness came up over him like night.

When he opened his eyes again he was lying on a down-soft bed, and there was a feeling in his head like strong Thanksgiving wine, and a tingling in his body that ran right down to his fingers and toes. The Shining One was sitting beside him, his appearance muted in the dimly lit room to a faint silver-gold. He held to Jody's face a strange cup, with a tube that led from it to a machine, like some of the Old Days things that littered the back of the shelter cave. He tried to drink from the cup, but whatever magic filled it was invisible and tasteless. He took a deep breath, and his chest and head were filled with a wonderful tingling. He no longer felt drowsy, but ravenously hungry and consumed with curiosity. His feet throbbed, but otherwise he felt wonderful. He tried to struggle up, and at once the Guardian took the cup away from his face and restored it to its holder on the machine.

"I will fetch you some food. Then when you have rested I will show you our home and take you to meet Olwen. Do not try to leave this room."

Jody looked up with a frown. Was he a prisoner then? But there was nothing but amusement in the cool voice that answered his unspoken thoughts. "No, Jody, you are not a prisoner. But I have made the air in this room thicker, so that you may be comfortable. Do you understand that? If you should attempt to leave by yourself the thick air will leak out of the room. Wait and be easy. I will not be long."

He walked with his strange stiff-legged gait to the wall in front of the bed. There was a hiss. The wall vanished and instantly reappeared again. The Guardian was gone!

Jody leapt to his feet, staggering as the pain in his feet shot up his legs. He stared at the wall, which was made of silky smooth stuff, harder than rock. He could make no mark on it either with a fingernail or with his knife. There was no seam, nor any way of seeing how it had opened and shut. Magic indeed . . .

He looked at the other three walls. They were made more

simply of Isis rock, smoothed in a way that no tools could ever match, and slicked over with a shine that looked wet to the eyes, but was dry to the touch of fingertips. Whether he was in a cave like the shelter cave in the valley, or in a house made of great slabs of rock, Jody could not tell. There were no windows, and the light came softly from squares in the high ceiling.

He looked wonderingly around. On the floor was a warm covering woven in an intricate design of flowers and birds, in colours far beyond the range of the leaf and berry and lichen that the women of Isis used for dyeing. There were purples as rich and dark as night, and greens that shimmered like the Northern Lights. It must have taken several lifetimes to weave, so fine and intricate it was.

The bed from which he had jumped was covered with fine cloth as silky as the mattress was soft, and there was cloth of the same kind draped about the head of the bed. It seemed to have no purpose, but it made the room look very grand. There was a low table with nothing on it set upon the carpet, and two chairs that looked so comfortable that he had to bounce in each of them to try them out.

Against the left wall was a storage unit, made by some master craftsman, for Jody barely had to touch the drawer-pulls for the drawers to slide out as smoothly as if they were oiled. They were all empty, which gave him the queer feeling that he was in a room that had never been used before.

He closed the drawers carefully and looked around again. The only thing he had missed was a door in the wall to the right of the bed. It was an ordinary door, with a knob, and though he longed to explore, he remembered what the Guardian had said about the air. He had better wait. He limped back to the middle of the room and stood waiting, more and more aware of the sweat and dirt that grimed his body, of his ragged clothes and the disaster that had once been his sandals.

By the time the Shining One reappeared through the magic wall, Jody was feeling very humble and ashamed. He bowed very low and then stood with his eyes down.

"What is the matter?" The Guardian placed a large tray on the table.

"Lord, I am not fit to be in a place like this. I am unwashed and my clothes are worn out."

"It is I who am at fault. The food can wait a few minutes. Come with me." He threw open the door at which Jody had hesitated, disclosing a small square room covered completely in pale, shining, slippery stuff. "Throw your clothes on the floor. Do not worry. I will make new ones for you."

Encouraged, Jody stripped off his filthy rags and stood shivering while the Shining One pressed knobs and turned levers and made warm scented water come out of the wall and wash the dust from his hair and body. He was given a handful of softness to rub over his body, which turned into a million sweet bubbles as he scoured his skin till it tingled. Finally the water went away and in its place there was warm air coming from the walls and ceiling that dried his skin, and then he was wrapped in a robe of stuff every bit as soft as the bed coverings.

Back in the room the Shining One desired Jody to sit, so, feeling very strange, Jody sat at the table while the Guardian took shiny silver lids off plates made of fine white clay and placed them one by one in front of Jody and commanded him to eat. It was not difficult to obey. The food was delicious, unlike anything he had tasted before. There was no meat, but the various vegetables were prepared in many different ways, with subtle sauces that made his mouth water for more.

When at last he had had enough, the Guardian made him stay sitting in his chair, while he took away the tray of dishes, to return with a smaller tray containing pots of ointment and a pile of white clothes. Then, in spite of his protests, the Guardian knelt at Jody's feet and dressed his cuts and blisters and sores, trimmed his broken nails and bandaged the sorest places.

"You should not, Lord," Jody protested.

The strange crystalline eyes looked up into his anxious brown ones. "Why not?"

"Because you are the Guardian of Isis."

"Is it not part of a guardian's duty to look after those in his charge?" was the reply.

The answer left Jody's head spinning. It was so different from what he had been taught. Surely to be Lord was to be boss. To be President, as Mark London was, was to be feared, to be obeyed, to be looked up to—not with love—with awe. The Guardian's idea was too large to think about now. It must wait, he decided, until he had recovered from all this strangeness and had time to think.

When Jody's cuts and blisters had been dressed, the Guardian measured his feet, picked up the tray and walked to the vanishing wall. "Rest now. I will return later."

Rest. Full, clean and comfortable, Jody tumbled onto the bed. He intended to lie and sort out all the new things that had happened to him, so that he might make some kind of sense and order of it all. But the warmth and the softness were too much for him and he slept.

He was wakened by the hiss of the magic wall. He blinked and struggled up on one elbow, muddled with sleep. Where was his room with the view of the lake? Where was his familiar bed, the chest, the hook for his clothes?

The pale light from the ceiling streamed down on the fine bed covers and the elaborate carpet. At the foot of the bed stood the Shining One, with a soft bundle which turned out to be trousers and a tunic, fitting Jody exactly, and a pair of slippers which the Guardian put carefully on his bandaged feet.

"But ... they are like my skin," Jody stammered. "They might have been made for me."

"They were."

Jody stared, and then looked down at his feet and wiggled his toes against the incomparable smoothness of the slippers' lining. "You are indeed the great and Shining One, Lord," he whispered.

"Tush! I am a maker, no more."

"I know. Lord. Maker of Isis and Ra and of the heavens themselves."

"No, no, no! I am a maker of *things*, not of worlds, boy. That you must try to understand. But do not worry. Olwen will explain it to you, all in good time. But no more bowing down. It is not fitting."

"Lord?"

"You may call me Guardian, simply, as she does. Nothing more. The true lord of Isis is my lady, the Keeper of the Isis Light. You may kneel to *her*. Now what is wrong?"

"That name..." Jody stammered, his dark face greying with unexpected fear.

"The Keeper? Then you have not forgotten, you know what it means?"

90

"Yes, indeed, Lord—Guardian, I mean. It is not a thing we speak of much."

"Nevertheless, you had better tell me."

Jody took a deep shuddering breath. "Before the Beginning Times there was the Shining One, who holds the worlds in his hands and governs the light of Ra. But then came That Old Woman, the Ugly One, and she stole the shining of Ra and made night and death and fear. So now there are two, as there are night and day, and heat and cold, and feasting and hunger, and birth and ... and death. And all these bad things came because she took the Light and would not give it back. And we call *her* the Keeper. Her place used to be with that strange *thing* on top of the mesa, but now she dwells in the north. And now her name is taboo, and we never use it, but call her That Old Woman, or sometimes the Ugly One, because she brings death to the people. But you bring life, and that is why we kneel to you and call you 'Lord'. You must know all this, yet you say that I must not kneel to you but to *her*, and call *her* Lord. Is night stronger than day then, and death stronger than life? If so, nothing that we do has any meaning any more!"

Jody's voice rose in a wail, and the Guardian, who had listened to his tumbling urgent words with a smooth impassive face, now leaned forward and gently shook his shoulders. "No, Jody. Stop! Listen to me. These are stories to frighten children, and there is little or no truth in them. You must not be afraid, or at least, for it is important that you do not hurt her feelings, I do not want you to show fear. Can you promise me that?'

"Not to fear the Ugly One, who is the darkness and the end of all things?" Jody's voice quavered.

"Do not call her Ugly. There is no truth in it." He had not heard the Guardian's voice so stern. He ventured to look into the smooth face. There was no anger to be seen, and the crystal-line eyes were as clear and bland as ever.

"But is she not...?"

"It is only a tale to frighten children. She is Olwen Pendennis, the Keeper of the Light, which is something very different from what you have been told; and though she is the most great lady on Isis, she is not to be feared, I promise you. Come. It is time that I took you to meet her. It seems that you have a great deal to learn, and perhaps even more to forget!"

Chapter Nine

Guardian led Jody past the vanishing wall, and he found himself in a narrow place, like a cupboard, with no furniture or decoration, and there they stood. Nothing seemed to happen except for a faint sound like the breathing of a giant a very long way off. Then that too ceased, and the wall in front of them vanished, in just the same way as the bedroom wall. The Guardian took Jody's arm and pulled him forward. There was a hiss behind him, and when he quickly turned, there was no longer a little room, but only a blank wall.

He turned again, to face a huge room, and would have walked forward to explore it, but Guardian touched his arm again. "The air here is too thin for you. You must remember to use this." He slung a satchel across Jody's shoulder, and showed him a cup, like the magic one that had been full of invisible wine, which he was to hold to his mouth and breathe from whenever he felt dizzy and tired.

"But this is what I wanted to invent," Jody said excitedly, after he had looked at it very carefully. "I had thought that if there was only a way of putting air into containers, then you could take it out when you needed it. Then our people would be able to climb the mountains, if we ever had to leave the Valley."

"That is good. But this is not air; it is oxygen, which is the part of air that you use for breathing."

"Could you show me how to catch it and store it?" Jody asked excitedly. Perhaps this was how the people were to be saved. If the Valley were to flood then they would have to take to the mountains...

"It's possible. We must see what Olwen has to say. It would not be wise to give you more than you can handle."

Jody could make no sense of that, so he turned again to gaze at the huge room in front of him. It was lit, not only by squares of light in the ceiling, but by high narrow windows cut in the far wall.

"May I look?" he asked, and the Guardian gestured as if giving him the freedom of the place. The room must have been thirty paces deep from where he stood, at the back, to the windows, and it was even wider. He wondered how many people it must have taken to build a house of such huge blocks of stone, and how long it must have taken. He limped slowly across the floor and peered out of one of the windows.

He was surprised to see that Ra was high. It had been Ra-down when he had met the Guardian. He must have slept the night and half the day, and yet it had felt like a few minutes. He leaned across the depth of stone sill, and found that he was looking, as a mountain eagle might look, across the width of the valley towards the western mountains.

Below him was a haze, almost like cloud, lying deep along the valley, and through it he could see faintly, like an endless silver snake, the river wriggling lazily from left to right. On this side of the river a continuously moving silver-grey shimmer puzzled him. It was like a giant waterfall, but wider than any waterfall could possibly be. After a while he realised that he was looking down through the misty air into the ancient grove of giant bamboos, but from such a height that the movement of the streamer-like leaves was transformed into the shimmer of water.

How high was he? It must be very, very high. He leaned further out across the stone sill until he could see the ground directly below. The world turned sickeningly around him. He felt like a tiny beetle clinging to a rock. Below him was nothing but space, and more space, until far, far below, through the mist that he began to realise was the atmosphere of the valleys of Isis, he picked out a jumble of scree and thornbush that skirted the foot of the mountain.

Where was this house—this palace? The coldness of the stone sill beneath his bare arms told him the giddy truth. This place was not built on a mountain—it was *in* the mountain. It was like the Sacred Cave, only so many times larger that he did not have the numbers to think of it; and instead of being at the foot of the mountain, it was at the very top, in upper Isis, so close to the sky that Jody felt sure that at night the fire of the stars must burn them.

He slid quickly back off the sill only to feel the solid floor turn under him, and the walls tilt, pushing him back towards the window, out into that horrible space. His fingers found the back of a chair, mercifully solid, and he clung to it with his eyes tightly shut.

"It is only vertigo. You will be better presently." The calm voice of the Guardian penetrated through the panic, and cool fingers unhooked the breathing cup and held it to his mouth and nose. In a while he was able to open his eyes again, and let go of the chair and take the breather in his own hands. But his stomach churned uneasily whenever he glanced towards the windows.

"You have never been on upper Isis before?"

"No." He swallowed and licked his dry lips. "No, Guardian. As you must know, the mountains and the mesa are taboo. If a man should break that taboo, the sudden sickness would take him to That Old Woman."

"Yet you wished to invent a breather to help you explore?"

"Yes, Lord."

"Go on. Tell me why."

"Well, I thought that if we had breathing things, then perhaps we would be able to live in the mountains, or at least explore the part of Isis that lies outside our Valley. I thought that maybe the taboo was a way of protecting us from the sudden sickness of the mountains, and that maybe ... but the President says that the taboos are there because they are there, and that it is not for us to question them or try to change anything."

"That is why you were not popular, then?"

"Yes, Guardian."

"And they sent you to us, without a breather or a suit? They must have known ... and yet you got here safely. There must be some kind of adaptation going on ... but so rapid?" He seemed to be talking to himself, and since Jody did not understand a word he was saying he stood silently. He was beginning to feel better, and started to look around the room once more, being careful to keep his eyes away from the windows.

The huge room was furnished sparsely, but with great elegance. If all the people of Isis had to be packed in this one room, it would have been crowded, but it could be done. He could not understand what the room was for. There were no looms nor spinning wheels, nor any kind of working tools. There was no dining table or benches, so it could not be a dining hall. There were fat comfortable-looking blocks, obviously intended for sitting on; and there were small low tables, some with a single vase of flowers.

There were paintings on the walls, and timidly at first, but then more freely when he saw that the Guardian did not mind, he began to walk around and look at them. Some of them he could recognise as scenes of Isis and studies of familiar flowers. But there were other, stranger pictures, that seemed to belong to the dream world of night. In these paintings a man's face recurred in some form or other. It was an unknown face, and yet in an odd way it was tantalisingly familiar.

He was still staring at the paintings when the Guardian turned his head alertly. "She is coming," he said softly, and in spite of his unemotional voice he reminded Jody of a man waiting for his love. He himself heard nothing, but he stood waiting politely until, twenty heartbeats later, a small figure swept regally into the room.

The Guardian walked quickly towards her. "Olwen, this is..."

"Jody?" She interrupted him and walked swiftly across the room until she was standing directly in front of him. "No, you're not Jody. You can't possibly be. Jody would be an old man, almost as old as I." Her hands flew to her face and she laughed, bewildered.

Jody had not even heard her. This was the lady Olwen? This was the one whom the Guardian, the Shining One, served and loved? He stared, repelled and attracted, disgusted and fascinated, all at the same time. Her face was broad, with wide nostrils and thick lips not unlike his own. The forehead, though high, was strangely shaped and bumpy. But these details were insignificant beside the one startling impossible fact that her skin was a deep and iridescent bronzy-green, and not smooth like a person's, but scaly like a snake's.

He stared, and became aware of her hair, which was very thick and wavy, flowing over her shoulders in a cascade of silver. Then he saw her eyes, beaming at him, and the rest became unimportant. They were brilliantly deeply blue, like the precious stone that they sometimes found wedged in a matrix of crimson rock. They were more beautiful, more intelligent, more alive than the eyes of any person or creature he had ever seen; and quite without conscious thought Jody dropped to his knees.

"Lady." He bowed his head, his thoughts tumbling chaotically. If *she* is That Old Woman, the Ugly One, he thought, then Death must be a joy and an honour, not something to be dreaded and avoided at all cost.

She made him rise, taking his hands in hands that were small and cool and frail, yet ended in strong curved nails like those of the Hobbit-creature. But the contradiction did not repel him.

"Jody?" she asked again, peering into his face. She was old, he suddenly realised, perhaps even as old as the President. For a moment her unlined face and thick white hair had fooled him.

"Yes, lady, I am Jody N'Kumo," he managed to say.

"But you cannot be. That was so many years ago ... how long, Guardian?" She turned for an instant to the Shining One who stood quietly watching her, but she did not wait for his reply, turning eagerly back to Jody. "Of course. He must be your father. That is the explanation."

"My father is named Isaac. But my grandfather, who is one of the Council of Seven, is called Jody also."

"Grandfather!" Her hands went to her face in a comical gesture of dismay. "So long ago? Is it possible, Guardian? Can it really be so long?"

"Perfectly possible, Olwen."

"Jody, you must forgive me for greeting you like this. But you remind me so much of your grandfather that I was startled. It was as if it had all happened yesterday. Yet now I look at you I see that you are not the same. Your skin is lighter and your hair is different. And of course you are much older. The Jody I knew was a very small boy, and you are almost a man, are you not?"

Jody's head spun. His grandfather had known the lady Olwen? Known and been loved by and remembered. And never a word in all the long years of story-telling. Never a word or a hint. WHY?

"Come, sit down here beside me, and tell me how your people are doing. Are they all well? Is your grandfather in good health? Can you believe that I knew him once when he was a mischievous little boy, getting into trouble? Years, oh, years younger than you. Come." She patted one of the big soft cubes and sank gracefully onto it, her gaily flowered robe falling into

96

meadowland folds around her. "Come, sit here."

Although he would have felt more comfortable kneeling at her feet, Jody did as he was told, and sat gingerly on the corner of the cube. It was very soft and so comfortable that he found himself sinking into it in a way that made it difficult to keep respectfully upright. The Lady Olwen made this even more difficult by taking one of his hands. "Tell me all about yourself," she invited him.

Jody found himself talking about his life, about the Fourths of his own age with whom it was so difficult to mix, and about the Thirds who were all old and married and full of sober responsibility. He told her about his dreams and inventions, and he made her laugh when he described what had happened when he had flown his kite in the thunderstorm. Then he told her about the President, and about the taboos and how life had to be lived without questioning anything he said. He even told her about the quarrel that lay so heavily between his grandfather and the President.

"And who is this sour man, and why do you keep him as your President, if he is like that?" the Lady asked.

"Mark London," he told her, and did not understand why her young face should suddenly look so old. "He is the oldest of the Firsts, you see, and he has been President of Isis for many many years, since long before I was born."

She smiled faintly at that, but she must have been tired, because she did not ask him any more questions. He wondered if he had done anything wrong, and whether he should leave her alone.

The same idea seemed to have occurred to the Guardian, for he stepped forward and spoke softly to her. "You are tired, Olwen. Rest, and I will look after the boy."

"No, oh no." She looked up and smiled as if her muscles found it hard to do. "I am not tired, Guardian dear. Only a little surprised to find that those old wounds still hold so much pain. I thought I had forgotten. But it is all right. I know what we will do—we will have a party for Jody. Oh, it has been so long! Guardian, do you remember my last birthday in Cascade Valley, and the party you made for me just before Pegasus Two landed? Oh, how long ago that was! I thought then that the whole world had turned upside down when they landed in the valley. Yet look at us now. Here we are, just you and I, as we always were, all these many years later. How strange! Yet I can remember it as if it had just happened."

"I too remember, Olwen; and I will go and prepare a party." He hovered above her. "You will not get overtired?"

"No, dear Guardian. I will not get overtired." She smiled up at him, and Jody saw the silver-gold hand clasp Olwen's shoulder, and her greenish hand rest for a minute on top of it. It was strange. They behaved the way very old friends do, or people who have been in love with each other for a very long time. Was the Guardian only a servant, as he had said? And how long had the two of them been on Isis?

Pegasus Two was the Beginning. That was clear from the legends. Before Pegasus Two there was nothing. Could these two really have been on Isis before then—in the Nothing time?

"I do not understand," he burst out, once the Shining One had glided from the room on silent silver-gold feet.

"What do you not understand, Jody?"

"Everything!"

"Oh, dear. That is a lot. But why? You must know about Guardian and me and our home here in Bamboo Valley. Perhaps we could start from there."

"But I don't know about it. About you. About this place. About the Shining One."

"Who is that? Do you mean...?"

"The Guardian of Isis." Jody's voice dropped. "He told me that he is your friend and servant. But yet he is the God of this place, is he not? That is what we were always taught. Yet I can see that you are friends. And *he* is going to make a party for *us*. It does not make any sense. If he, who is the Lord of Isis and Ra and everything, is your friend and servant, then what are you, Lady?"

"Oh, dear. Time has muddled up the truth." Laughter and tears seemed to be mixed in her voice. "Jody, I will tell you a shameful secret about myself. Once upon a time, oh, so many years ago that I have forgotten, I thought that I *was* the most important person in the world, and I truly believed that all of Isis belonged to me. Guardian was with me then. He has always been with me, ever since my parents were killed and left me in his care. And you are quite right. He *is* my friend, although he

98

likes to think of himself as my servant, and is most happy when he is doing something or making something for me. Which is why this house, although it is only for the two of us, is so large and splendid. It is Guardian's way of saying—I love you. He does not know how to say it any other way."

Jody's eyes were fixed on her face. He had decided by now that she was very beautiful. "Go on. *Did* you own Isis? What happened?"

"No, it was never mine. That was only a childish vanity. After my parents died Guardian and I between us kept the Light and sent out the signals into the Galaxy every day, as we had to do. I had him and he gave me everything I wanted. I did not know what it was to be lonely, because I had never known any other kind of life. Then one day, just after my birthday, everything changed. Pegasus Two landed and your grandfather and his parents and all the other settlers were here, eighty of them. Once I got over being angry because Isis was no longer all mine, I hoped to be friends with the new people. But it did not work out that way. My job as Keeper of the Light was finished, and they did not really need me. So Guardian and I left your people in Cascade Valley, and came here."

"Were you happy to leave?" Jody asked, and she looked at him strangely.

"It was difficult at first," she said after being silent for a while. "I had discovered loneliness, you see, which is the other side of love. And I was in love then. But it passed in time. The years have been pleasant, and I have always had Guardian. But it is very good to see another person, Jody, and especially you. Of all my memories of your people, the ones I have of your grandfather are the only ones that are without pain. I know it is difficult for you to breathe on upper Isis, but I do hope that you will stay with us for a while. We will try to make you comfortable."

"I shall be glad to stay for as long as you want me, Lady. And it is not *too* difficult to breathe up here," he lied. Then he spoiled it by asking, "Lady, why do you choose to live so high, when you have the whole valley spread out empty below you? The valley is beautiful, and up here the air is so thin one's chest hurts. Are not the mountains taboo to you?"

"Nothing should be taboo on Isis, not for anyone. Something has gone very wrong to make it so. There is no wrong in it; it is just that living on the heights can be dangerous for Earth people."

"But not for you?"

"No, not any more. You must understand, Jody, that I too am of Earth stock. But when my parents, who were the first Keepers of the Light, were killed in a storm, long before the coming of Pegasus Two, Guardian changed me so that it would be safe for me to live anywhere on Isis, in the valleys or on the heights. He made me so that I can breathe comfortably up here, and he made my skin the way it is so that the ultra-violet rays of Ra will not damage me. Do you understand? I can go anywhere I choose, but I am happiest up high, where the air is clear and sweeps around the length and breadth of beautiful Isis."

Jody found the Lady Olwen's careful explanations every bit as confusing as his previous ignorance. "What is the Keeper of the Light? The Guardian told me that we were mistaken in our stories about it. And what is ultra-violet and why does it hurt? I have never seen it, I think. It is not a word I have ever heard before."

It was her turn to stare. "Your people have not even kept the memory of those who lived alone on Isis and kept the signals going out into the whole Galaxy until Earth was ready to send out settlers?" She sounded deeply offended. "My parents gave their lives exploring Isis to make sure that it was safe for *you*."

"I am sorry. We were never taught that. What is the Light?"

"It is the metal thing at the top of Lighthouse Mesa. It still sends out messages, only now it is just an automatic signal."

Jody nodded. "The mesa is one of the taboos, you see. And so is the god-thing at the top."

"It is not a god-thing . . ." She stopped and sighed. "Well, never mind that now. But you must understand about ultra-violet, to have survived safely all this time. Perhaps you have a different word for it. You must know that Ra, besides giving us light and heat, also gives off other invisible rays that are dangerous to human beings. That is why you must wear special suits when you climb the mountains. Your valley is the lowest place on Isis, and the air there is thick enough to protect you from the ultra-violet. Do you understand?"

"I think so. It is from Ra that the thing called the mountain

100

sickness comes, that you will get if you break the taboo and climb the mountains. But of course we never do."

"You haven't used the UVO suits and explored the other valleys?"

"I do not know what a UVO suit is."

"But, Jody, you came over the high passes to get here..."

"He was wearing less than you see on him now," the Guardian interrupted. He had returned quietly with an enormous tray piled with dishes which he began to set out carefully on one of the low tables.

"Truly? He is not sick? Guardian, have you checked him over?"

"Do not worry, Olwen. I scanned him fully while he was asleep. There was some sunburn, and a little fluid in the lungs. Nothing that could not easily be taken care of."

"I don't understand. How did he manage to get here safely?"

"His dark skin protected him. If his people came originally from the highlands of Africa he would acclimatise more quickly than is usual. It seems likely."

"Where does your family come from, Jody?"

He spread his hands, embarrassed at the stupidity of the question. "From Isis, Lady Olwen. Where else?"

"I mean before that. It is not so many generations ago. Do you never talk about Earth?"

"Of course. The Thanksgiving Day story. Earth is that little star over in the west in the notch between the two big peaks... only that is in *our* Valley, not here. The story says we came from Earth on a ship called Pegasus, which is also the name of a great winged beast called a horse. It is only a story, you understand. A ship cannot really sail through the air, nor can a horse. And that star is either too little to live on, or it is large and hot and too far away. Really we come from Isis, Lady."

Olwen turned to Guardian, her eyes shocked. "How can a people forget its own history so fast? All the knowledge, the science ... Guardian, what has happened?"

"It has been made to happen deliberately, Olwen. I cannot understand why, though I can guess. But who caused it to happen, of that I *am* sure. Do you know who is still the President of the settlement?"

"Yes." She bit her lip and turned away from them both,

101

silent, abstracted. Jody could feel her pain, but he did not know what he could do to help.

Guardian made a sudden clatter among the dishes, and begged pardon in a low voice. Jody looked up, puzzled. He was sure that the Shining One was never clumsy or made mistakes like that.

The Lady Olwen started at the sound, turned and came back to them. "Our party! I had almost forgotten. Come, Jody dear. I hope you are hungry. Guardian likes to make the most stupendous feasts, and I no longer have the appetite I had when I was a girl. So you must do this spread justice, or he will be offended." It was said with a laugh, and Jody thought he caught an answering gleam in the Guardian's crystalline eyes.

She sat at the low table. Jody hesitated. There were only two chairs drawn up to it. "Sit here, Jody. Come," she urged him.

"But what about the Guardian?" he asked bluntly.

"Guardian's energy is renewed by Ra. He has no need of food."

"Then he *is* a God. Yet you allow him to serve you?"

"It is his pleasure. Believe me, that is true. And he is no God. I will explain it all to you when we have eaten the feast, and you have told me why you came on this perilous journey."

Jody sat down then, and after staring at the heaped platters with popping eyes he began to dig in. The Lady Olwen sat, toying with the food on her own plate, but with laughter in her eyes as she watched him demolish the elegant feast.

She did not speak until he pushed back his chair with a sigh. "That was the best meal I have eaten in my whole life," he declared, and when she passed him another dish he shook his head. "No, thank you. I couldn't. I'm much too full. Why does this taste so very different from the food *we* eat?"

"What do you eat?"

"Oh, barley and fish stew, and baked rock bunnies when we can catch them, but they are getting fewer. And bread, of course, and berries. And once in a great while honey. But usually, you see, the bees make their nests too high, where we are not allowed to go."

"Who makes the rules and says where you may and may not go?"

"The Council of Seven. Angus McCann, Will Bodnar,

102

Patrick Connelly, Grant Nolan, Lars Holmstrom, my grandfather, and the President—Mark London. Mostly it is the President who makes all the rules and the others just go along with what he says. I don't know if it's supposed to be that way, or if it is because that is the kind of men they are. It doesn't make much sense to me, because that way you don't get any different ideas."

"It makes no sense to me either. Nor can I imagine a person like your grandfather 'going along with' anything he did not feel was right. Unless he has changed a great deal since the days when I knew him."

Jody grinned. "He hasn't changed. But he seldom attends the meetings. He and Mark London quarrelled badly many years ago, and since he was so badly crippled..."

"Crippled? Jody!" she cried, and he knew she did not cry his name, but that other boy's that she knew so long ago. "Could the doctor do nothing to help him?"

"Doctor?"

"Oh, what was his name?... MacDonald, that was it, Philip MacDonald. He was a very good doctor."

"Did you know him? He died not long ago. He was one of the elders. They do no work, of course."

"No work? What nonsense. Surely they teach, advise?" Jody shook his head, and she went on. "But he must have passed his knowledge on to someone else? Babies are born. People have falls or hurt themselves working. Who looks after them?"

"Babies are part of women's magic and I know nothing about that. But from a fall or a cut a person either gets better or he goes to That Old Woman."

"What do you mean?"

Jody stared at her with wide eyes. "You *must* know. I thought you were She, at first. Before we met."

"Explain, please."

"That Old Woman who is the Ugly One. She who takes us from this good life to that other place."

"Death?"

Jody nodded. "She is much to be feared. But the Shining One, the Guardian, from whom She stole the Light, he protects us and sends us Gifts, even now, although we no longer hear his voice in the Sacred Cave."

103

He would have gone on, but he saw that she was no longer listening to him, but staring up at the Shining One with pain and bewilderment in her beautiful eyes. "Could Mark really have twisted the truth so much?" she whispered.

"If he was full of anger and shame. It would be easier to change reality than to face it as it was," the Guardian answered.

"He was not *bad*. A little selfish. But not *evil*," she burst out.

"Perhaps not intentionally evil. He started out with only a small lie, to make himself feel more comfortable. And then a bigger lie, laid on the first one, like a stone on a wall. And then another. Until now, after all these years, it has become a whole building."

"An ugly lying building. We must tear it down, Guardian."

"Be careful, Olwen. Do not act out of hurt. Wait until the pain goes away a little and you can see how to act with wisdom."

She sighed and stood up slowly, as if she was suddenly much older. "Thank you, dear Guardian. You always know."

He inclined his head stiffly. "I can only advise. Yours is the wisdom. Wait until you find it."

"I will. I need to be alone now. I think I will climb up to my cave. Look after Jody, Guardian, and find out from him why he came north."

"Lady!" Jody called as she reached the door. She turned in a swirl of fabric. "I don't understand," he stammered. "You knew our President once ... I thought ... but you sound now as if you hate him."

"Hate him?" She smiled wrily. "Oh, no, Jody. Once I was in love with Mark London and I believed that he loved me. I could never hate him."

Chapter Ten

After the Lady Olwen had gone Jody stared at the door through which she had vanished. *She* had loved the President? He tried to imagine Mark London without his flowing beard, his long white hair, without the forbidding frown and the beak of a nose jutting out from his bony forehead. But he couldn't. It was not just that the President was *old*. After all, the Lady Olwen was old too, but in a different way. It was simply the fact that the President was not lovable.

He had been married, of course. All the men and women on Isis were married. But Mark London's wife had been dead for many years and he lived with his sons and their wives. The sons were all remarkably silent men, and as for their wives, they were cowed and downtrodden.

The Lady Olwen had spoken of change, as if something bad had happened to the people of Isis. Perhaps that kind of change could happen to a single person too. Perhaps Mark London, the boy, had been a very different person from Mark London, the man. Yet not everybody changed that way with age. He could still recognise in his crippled grandfather the mischievous boy of whom the Lady Olwen spoke with such affection.

Because he knew how to invent machines that sometimes worked, even though everyone else laughed at them, Jody had begun to feel that he was a great deal cleverer than the Fourths and even than the other Thirds, old and married though they were. But now he suddenly saw, in a plunge into depression, that he knew *nothing*. After all, machines were easy to understand. But people were a mystery!

He frowned, watching the Guardian pile a tray with the remains of the feast, whisk away a few crumbs and place a bowl of flowers on the table.

"There is so much I don't understand," he cried out impatiently. "Guardian, can you explain to me what is happening?"

The Guardian hesitated, and moved the bowl of flowers in a finicky way a hair's breadth to one side. "I do understand about

Olwen and Mark London. But that is Olwen's affair. It is for her to explain to you if she should wish to do so. As for the changes that have happened to your people, I lack a few facts which you can probably supply. An exchange of information should prove mutually beneficial."

"Huh?"

"You tell me about the Isis you know, and I'll tell you about it the way I know it. Do you understand?"

"Of course. Who'll begin first?"

"You, if you please. Repeat the story from your beginnings, if you will."

Jody stood upright and began to recite. "I am Jody, son of Isaac N'Kumo, grandson of Jody N'Kumo, who is one of the Council of Seven. I am a Third—the youngest of them, not old enough to marry. Even some of the Fourths are older than I am."

Guardian raised a golden hand. "Would it be correct to surmise that your father is a Second and your grandfather a First?"

Jody stared. "Of course."

"Then what of *his* father?"

"Grandfather's...? Oh, he would have been an elder if he were still alive."

"How many elders remain?"

"Fifteen."

"I understand that the Council under the President rules the people of Isis, but what do the elders do?"

"Do? Why, nothing. They are very old."

"But still ... advice ... stories of the old days...?"

"Oh, no." Jody was shocked. "The stories are told us by the Council. We honour the elders and look after them, but we don't listen to them. The Council says that their ideas are old-fashioned and unsuitable for life on Isis."

"The Council? Or the President?" the Guardian put in softly.

Jody thought back. He remembered the tens of low-voiced arguments between Grandfather and Grandmother in the old days. Though Grandmother always stood up for what her brother did, under the surface he felt that all was not well between them. But that was only a feeling. On the surface she used to shush Grandfather every time he burst out with one of his 'blast that proud fool Mark. Does he really believe that he can change history?'. But that was long ago, and maybe he had got the words muddled. But he told the Guardian what he thought he remembered anyway.

The Guardian seemed to understand. He nodded his smooth head slowly. "I would like to know more of the ways in which the President changed history. Can you tell me?"

Jody shrugged. "I never understood what they meant. This was long ago, when I was little."

"All right. Tell me more about your beginnings."

"The Thanksgiving story? In the beginning, long long ago, when the world was young, men and women came in a ship through the sky from a world called Earth, and they settled on Isis, in the Valley. They lived there and had many children and the Guardian blessed..." He choked and stopped. It was one thing to tell the stories, but quite another to relate one's beginnings in front of the Shining One himself. "But you know all this, Lord," he stammered at last, and stared bashfully at the ground.

"It would please me to hear it, just as it was taught you."

"Very well, Lord. The ... the Guardian blessed the Valley and the grain and the fruits and the fish in the lake and all the animals in the Valley, that the people might use them. But on the mountains and on the mesa that is in the Valley he set a curse, so that they are now taboo. If anyone should break that taboo they will sicken and die and go to That Old Woman."

"Is anything else taboo?"

"Oh, many things. The Sacred Cave is taboo, except to those whose duty it is to keep vigil there. And your Gifts which are kept there are also taboo, I think, but I am not certain." Jody remembered the President's anger at him, but he still did not feel that he had done anything wrong.

"The Sacred Cave?"

"Where your voice was once heard, Lord."

"Do you hear it no more then?"

"You must know that, Lord. You have not spoken to us for many many years."

In the silence that followed his words Jody wondered if he had offended the Shining One. He could not tell. The smooth

107

face did not change. At last the Guardian spoke. "Then you have not used my Gifts?" he asked.

"Lord?" Guiltily Jody remembered how he had replaced the white wand in the ceiling and made the light come back. Was it possible for the Guardian to see right inside him and know the thing he had done, the crime for which he had been cast out of the Valley?

It seemed that he could. "Tell me the truth, Jody," he said quietly.

"Lord, I am sorry. Please do not send me to That Old Woman."

"What did you do?"

"I made the light come back inside the Cave," he whispered, and waited with his head bowed for the wrath to crack down upon him.

When it came it was not directed to him at all. "The fools! After all these years! About time! And what of my other gifts?"

"They are all safely stored in the Sacred Cave. No one has touched them," Jody hastened to reassure him.

"None used? Not even the water gauge?" The Guardian moved suddenly and Jody flinched in spite of himself. The Guardian drew back and stared at him. "Are you afraid of me?"

"Yes. Lord. Of course."

"Don't be. I'm not worth it," was the surprising answer. Then, as if to himself, the Shining One muttered, "How could I have been so *wrong*."

"Lord?"

The silver-gold figure turned quickly to him. "You do have the water gauge. It has been found? You know what it is for?"

Jody forgot the sacredness of the shining figure in front of him. His mind boiled with the triumph of being right after all. "It is to measure the rising water, isn't it? And if it goes above the red mark there is some kind of danger—there is something we must do? I told them. But no one would listen. No one paid attention when I warned them about the water. The President said that he was sending me to you to ask what should be done, but he did not mean it, I know, nor did he expect me to find you. He believed that That Old Woman would find me first. Even *he* didn't understand. What will we do if the Valley floods, Lord? Where will we go?"

"The Valley will not flood if I can help it. Do not be afraid for your people. Though I am not absolutely sure of the cause I can make an assessment that is 98.23% accurate." He stopped and looked at Jody who was staring at him open-mouthed. "You don't understand, do you?"

"No, Lord."

"It is my fault. I will explain it in your terms. You know the place where the river flows from Lost Creek into the ground?"

"It is the Place behind the Wall. I have never seen it."

The Guardian nodded. "The wall, of course, built by the settlers to guard against any more of their youngsters falling down the holes. You do know the story?"

Jody shook his head.

"You do not know that your own grandfather, when he was a very small boy, back in the first year on Isis, fell down one of the sink holes near Lost Creek?"

"Grandfather? He broke *that* taboo?"

"There *was* no taboo. There should be none now. It is a simple story. He was a curious child and he went exploring and got trapped in one of the holes. There was a bad storm coming, and when the people went to shelter in Pegasus—I had not made the cave for them then—they found he was missing. Olwen risked her life to find him and take him to the safety of the ship."

"And that is all?"

"That is all. The taboo is another nonsense of your President, I suspect. It was Olwen who rescued your grandfather, you see."

"No, I don't. It makes no sense at all. I wish you could explain."

"That is up to her. Now, about the wall. Have you never climbed it to see what lay beyond?"

"No, Lord, never."

"When you left your Valley to come here, did you look back from the top of the Cascades?"

"Not then, Lord. But when I found your Gift . . ."

"Then you saw behind the wall. You could not have helped yourself."

"I didn't. I didn't. I knew I mustn't look. Truly, Lord, I saw nothing!"

"Look at me." The soft voice was suddenly stern and Jody

looked up, startled. He found his eyes fixed to the crystalline eyes of the Shining One. He tried to move his gaze away, but he could not. From what seemed like a very long way off he heard the Guardian's voice. "Jody, you are at the top of the Cascades, looking down into your Valley. Do you see the river flowing towards the lake?"

Astonished, and yet calm, Jody saw. "Yes. I see it."

"It is misty down there, but from the far end of the lake you can see the river flowing in slow loops across the marsh towards the south."

"Yes."

"You see the circle of the wall, with the river vanishing into the place within. And there within the wall you see...?"

"Water. There is nothing but water there. Another lake enclosed by the Wall. That's all it is."

"Thank you, Jody." The Guardian spoke briskly and Jody blinked and looked shyly away. Had he been staring? What must the Shining One think of such bad manners?

"You were about to tell me what lay behind the wall," the Guardian went on matter-of-factly.

"Nothing but water, like another lake, right up to the Wall. Oh, how did I know that? I swear I never looked, Lord. I would not break that taboo of all taboos."

"There is no taboo. There never was. There are just games that the President has been playing. It is I, the Guardian of Isis, who tell you this."

"Thank you, Lord. But I do not understand."

"What do you not understand, Jody?"

"Why the things we were taught as children to be taboo are not taboo after all. Are our lives nothing but lies?"

"No, of course not. But in some areas ... yes, you have been misled."

"Why? By whom?"

The Guardian seemed to hesitate and Jody looked up in surprise. The beautiful face gave nothing away, but Jody sensed an unfamiliar awkwardness.

"You must know, Shining One. You know all things."

"Perhaps. Only it is not for me to tell you, but Olwen, if she should choose to."

Later that day Jody found himself back on the comfortable valley floor, where he could breathe without the help of bottled air. When he looked up at the mountainside he could see the small square shadows that were the doors and windows of the house where he had eaten and slept. It was hard to believe that he had been so high, higher than an eagle's eyrie. He shut his eyes and looked away, suddenly dizzy again at the memory of his descent from those awesome heights.

He had been persuaded towards the entrance, clinging frantically to the Guardian's arm. There had been a kind of platform overhanging the abyss, and on it stood a small thing with seats. He was made to climb into this thing, sweating and sick at the fear of the depths around him, and the Guardian had had to pry his fingers away from his golden arm.

The Lady Olwen had climbed into the thing beside him, and somehow he felt a little better. She made him close his eyes, and as he clung to the sides of the box-thing in which he sat he felt a trembling around him, as if the very mountain was shaking. Then there was a great quiet and a wind in his hair and on his face, and he nearly opened his eyes again, but he did not dare because he was sure that a very great magic was happening.

Then there was no movement and no wind, but only the scent of hot grass, and when the Lady Olwen told him to open his eyes he saw that he was no longer on the ledge at the top of the mountain, but at its foot, with the grove of bamboos behind him making their slow solemn music.

He scrambled out of the magic chariot and would have knelt to the Lady Olwen, but she would not let him. "It is only a floater," she had told him. "Made to run by the power of Ra. Your people had them too, in the beginning. I wonder what they have done with them?"

He could not answer her, and when she saw that he was still shaken by his magic journey she made him walk with her through the silvery moving shade of the bamboo grove, and then sit on the short turf by the little river to share their supper. Only when they had eaten did the Lady Olwen begin to explain to Jody the many things that had puzzled him.

At first it seemed hard for her to tell him, but gradually the words seemed to come more easily. "I have already told you that many years ago, when I was the same age as you are now, I lived alone on Isis with Guardian, who was my friend, my teacher, my companion. I was very happy, and I thought that my life was going to go on like that for ever. But then, when Pegasus Two arrived from Earth with eighty settlers, including twenty children, everything changed. Your President, Mark London, was the oldest of those children, and your grandfather Jody was the youngest."

He opened his mouth in protest, but she silenced him with a wave of one green-skinned hand. "Hush now. You will understand when I have finished. For now, listen. The settlers built the village where you live now. From the beginning, things went wrong. They would not speak to Guardian, or take his advice, and they insisted that I be part of their Council meetings.

"Guardian had not expected this attitude. He did not think that I would have to meet them so soon. He lied. To protect me from the disgust and scorn of the settlers he deceived both them and me; and from that one deceit terrible things rose. You have to understand that when Guardian changed me to suit the climate of Isis he made me into what I am, a person inhuman and disgusting. I could live anywhere on Isis; but I could not live with other human beings, because they could not tolerate me."

"Lady, I have to say something," Jody interrupted.

"Very well."

"When did the Guardian change you back?"

She stared at him. Then her hands fluttered to her face in a gesture that was totally human. "Oh!" She laughed uncertainly. "Jody, he has not changed me. Nothing has altered me but time."

"But you are beautiful. You could never have been disgusting. Never!"

She sighed. "Our eyes all have the same mechanism, yet each of us sees so differently. Guardian was afraid that the attitude of the settlers would hurt me, so he made a mask for me, so that I looked somewhat more like them. I went to meet them, and I would have gone to their councils, as they asked, and helped and advised them. Only . . ." She stopped, and then went on again. "Only I fell in love with Mark London, and I thought he loved me. But it was not so. He loved the mask. The lie. Not the real *me* that was behind the mask. He only saw me once as I really was, and he was so horrified and disgusted that the sight of me almost destroyed him. Guardian had been right to hide me from them. After that I stayed away and refused to wear the mask again."

She stopped talking, and Jody glanced shyly up at her. Her heavy brows were drawn together in a frown, as if the memories were recent and still too painful to bear. He had no words to tell her how he felt. He wasn't even sure that he knew how he felt. But he put out his scratched hand with its ragged nails, and touched hers. Its greenness, the colour of a bronze lizard, was attractive, and the texture was warm and dry.

She looked down, as if surprised, and before he could take his hand away, afraid that he had perhaps been too presumptious, she had put her other hand over his. Her strange eyes shone very brightly. Then she blinked, not the way a human blinks, but like a reptile. "Forgive me, Jody. I have not felt the loving touch of another human, besides Mark's, since I was a very small child."

"But the Shining One ... he is not human then? He is a god after all? But you said not, and so did he, and he acts as if he were your servant."

She smiled, squeezed his hand, released it and then blew her nose in a very ordinary way. "Now that I understand that Mark has made you all forget about your true beginnings, I can see why you are puzzled. You must understand that Guardian is my true friend because he has done and been all that a friend can do or be; but he still thinks of himself as a servant because that was what he was built to be."

"Built?" Jody swallowed. Was she mad? The Shining One *built*? Like a machine? Perhaps she was That Old Woman after all. If so, where could he run? People seldom cheated her for long, and in the end, never. He was suddenly sickeningly afraid.

At his sudden withdrawal and fear an expression came into her eyes that puzzled him. Could it be pain? But only human beings felt pain. His thoughts tumbled every which way like thorn bushes in a storm, and he could make no sense of any of them.

"You built the Shining One?" he asked after a long silence.

"Lady, I must ask you this. Are you the Maker or the Destroyer?"

"Neither." She looked at him, shocked. "God made the universe and everything in it. And there is no Destroyer."

"There may not be one in this valley. But there is in mine. I have seen her work. I have seen people die. Not only the elders, but grown people and even babies. That Old Woman took them..."

"Who?"

"The Ugly One. The Destroyer." He looked at her out of the corner of his eye. Was she? Wasn't she?

It *was* pain that he saw in her face. Pain and a terrible anger. She stood suddenly and left him sitting, and she walked to and fro as though she must get rid of her anger through movement rather than words.

After a time she came back. "There is no Destroyer," she said again. "There is no Ugly One, no Old Woman. Death is a door through which we must all pass, to be sure. But it is not an end, any more than the chrysalis that you see, torn and empty, hanging from a cactus spine, is the end. True, there is no more caterpillar. But see what there is instead. A beautiful moth, free to fly all over Isis and sup from the nectar of the golden cactus flower, instead of crawling on its belly with its nose to the ground, blindly chewing cactus spines."

Her voice rang with truth. He had to believe her. A load of fear and superstition fell from his shoulders, and he felt suddenly light enough to fly. "You are the moth, then, Lady?" he asked her, but she shook her head.

"Oh, no. Not yet. Like you, Jody, I am still working and waiting. I am different, but I am still human. The Guardian, though, is not. He is what used to be called a robot, which is a machine made to think and move and talk and do special complicated tasks."

"A machine? Like a floater?" His voice was scornful. He couldn't help it. It sounded so ridiculous.

"More like the computer in the cave. Do you understand?"

Jody shook his head. "He acts like a person."

"He was made to do that. Long ago, when my parents first came to Isis to set up the Light, they brought Guardian with them. He was not called Guardian then. His name was Dacop

114

43, and he was designed as a data collector and processor, especially adapted for the exploration of new planets. When my parents were killed in a rockfall, my mother lived long enough to reprogram Dacop 43. She taught him how to be my guardian, how to be loving and kind and protective, while still being as clever as he had always been."

"But he's not a human?"

"No."

"And he's not a god?"

"Absolutely not!"

"Will he die and change into something more beautiful?"

There was a glint of tears in her eyes when she answered. "Guardian will not die, and he cannot change. That is the difference between us, really the only difference that matters. I wish..." She stopped abruptly, and when she began to talk again Jody had the feeling that it was not what she had originally intended to say. "You see, Guardian is made of material that will never wear out, and if anything should go wrong with him he has the ability to fix it himself. He will last as long as Isis—longer, if he should choose to leave and go to some other star system."

"Do you think he would do that?"

"I don't know. I think not. I cannot bear to think what will happen to him when I am gone. He assures me that he cannot experience sorrow or loneliness or pain, but I..."

"How could he be so wise if he did not?" interrupted Jody.

"Exactly. He is much more human now than he was. You thought he was a person, didn't you? But of course you had never heard of robots, so you could not guess."

Jody had the feeling that the foundation of his world had been tumbled to the ground, the way a storm might tumble the bamboo poles of a house. When that happened, there was nothing to do but pick up the pieces and rebuild the house. This time, he promised himself, his world was not going to be built on lies. "If the Shining One is not truly the Maker and Guardian of Isis, then what is the meaning of the Gifts he has given us, and what is the Sacred Cave for?"

"Yes, it is important for you to know that. I told you that after Mark and I parted I decided that I would rather leave Cascade Valley and live up here. The settlers did not want me, and I did not want to see them, and be reminded every day of what I was. But I was still Keeper of the Light, and I had an obligation to them. I could not let them come to harm. So Guardian made two caves at the foot of Lighthouse Mesa, one to shelter your people from cosmic storms, and the other to house a communicator and computer. All the information you needed for your life on Isis was stored there, and if you needed help you could get in touch with either the Guardian or me. But we left you alone, except to give you warnings of cosmic storms and anything else that might affect your life and safety on Isis."

"That was the red light at the top of the cabinet?"

"That is only a small part of it. Over the communicator we were able to talk with your people and you with us. Then, some years after I had left, you stopped using the communicator. Guardian brought a floater into your valley to see if you were in any kind of trouble and he was warned off."

"Who would do such a thing?"

"Mark London. He had just been elected President. Yes, he warned us off, from our own planet! Can you imagine it? He said that he wished his people to develop without outside interference of any kind. So we respected his wishes, up to a point. We kept away from you, and we kept passing ships away from you also. We didn't even spy on you, which would have been easy enough to do. But the computer needed replacement parts; and over the years there were a few other things that seemed needful. Guardian left them for you at the top of the Cascades, where you would be able to find them, and use them if you wished."

"The magic wand that I put in the ceiling . . . was that one of those things?"

"Yes. And there was a micro-circuit replacement for the communicator. We had hoped that you would use it, so that we could warn you about the danger of the river."

"So the Valley will flood! And what is to become of us?"

"Something will be done, even if I have to come back among you myself, though I hope that will not be necessary. I am old now, Jody, and I do not think I could bear the fear and disgust any more. But if I must, I will."

Jody looked at the strangely-shaped face and the green-bronze skin, as scaly as a lizard's, and tried to see her as if he

116

were a stranger, but he could not, because her eyes, clear and intensely blue despite her age, looked at him unwaveringly, and he knew that the outside wasn't of any importance at all. He knew too that she would keep her word, that he could put all his trust in her and she would never let him down.

He drew a sigh of unconscious relief. "Can you tell me how the river actually began to flood? Guardian used long words and numbers and I didn't understand him at all."

"The river has always been a puzzle. It was the puzzle that attracted your grandfather and got him into trouble when he was a small boy." She smiled suddenly. "I too. When I was little one of my nightmares was that the river was pouring into a big hole under the ground, and that when the hole was quite filled up the river would begin to fill the valley, and then all the other valleys, and start climbing up the mountains, until all of Isis was drowned. But of course that was only a bad dream. There is not that much water on Isis. When Guardian found out what was bothering me he explained that the river found its way underground through a volcanic vent, and then seeped through faults and cracks until the pressure built up under Isis. Then, far away, on the side of some other mountain to the south, it was forced up and out to become another spring and start a new river, make a new beginning. And so on, over and over, round the planet, just as the egg becomes the skylark that lays the egg."

Jody nodded. It felt right and true. Not like the stories he had been brought up on that came up against the blank mountain wall of taboos instead of the open valley of answers. He thought about what she had told him. "But something went wrong?" he ventured.

"Yes. Not long ago Guardian was visiting a valley far to the south, beyond Cascade Valley, and he saw that all the northern streams and rivers had dried up. There had been ground tremors just before his visit—that was why he was there; and he suspects that some little shrug inside Isis has closed off the main vent through which your river used to flow. It would have been better if he could have gone into your valley and helped your people clear the vent before the water got too deep, but he was not able to do that. Your President would not have allowed it. All he could do was to talk to you over the communicator and warn you of what was happening. But there was no answer, so

117

we had no idea if you were even listening. So then he put the water gauge at the place above the Cascades, as a hint. He hoped that the President would realise that his pride might be the end of his people."

"I tried to explain about the gauge but the President wouldn't listen."

"I suppose his pride was greater than his love for you all." She looked very unhappy.

"Couldn't the Guardian have done something more?"

"Every day he has called you on the communicator."

"We have not heard his voice since long before I was born, Lady."

"No wonder, if you never replaced the worn-out circuit," she snapped. He was silent, and she went on more gently. "I am sorry, Jody. It is not your fault. It is not even entirely Mark's fault. If I had not misled him with that foolish mask . . . but that is in the past, and it is the *now* that we must worry about. How far has the water risen?"

"The Place behind the Wall is all water, and the lake is spreading, right up to the spot where the river enters it, where the stepping stones are?" He looked at her enquiringly.

She nodded. "Yes, Jody. I remember."

He stared at her. "You loved it, didn't you?" he asked, and at the expression on her face went on boldly. "But still you left?"

"I could no longer endure to live in the same place as Mark and the men who had killed Hobbit."

"Hobbit? That one?" His head spun at the thought of immortal monsters.

"No, no. His ancestor. As my Jody is yours." She sighed. "It is all a very long time ago. Anger passes. The fires go out, even though the scars of the burning remain. My whole happy childhood was spent in Cascade Valley and on Lighthouse Mesa. It was agony to turn my back on it all. When something reminds me, it is surprising to feel that the pain is still there, after all this time."

"You should never have left."

"I think perhaps you are right. If I had stayed I might have been a check, a balance. But at the time it seemed the best choice. How could I possibly guess how successfully Mark would destroy the past, even at the risk of the whole settlement?" Jody

118

knew that she was no longer talking to him at all.

After a while he said, "Can we stop the river from rising any more?"

"The river could be diverted away from your valley. But then you would have no more fresh water, and after a time the lake would become stagnant and the fish would die. I am sure that Guardian will have a better plan. *Guardian?*"

She spoke, it seemed to Jody, to the air, not even raising her voice, and he was startled almost out of his skin when the voice of the Shining One answered her, tiny, close by and invisible.

"Yes, Olwen."

"I think Jody is ready. We need your counsel. Will you come?"

Jody expected to see him appear, just like that, from among the giant bamboos; but nothing happened, and he let out his breath in a great sigh.

She saw his face and laughed. "It is not magic, nor are we gods, Jody. It is only a communicator, a small cousin of the one in your Sacred Cave." She showed him the ornate bracelet on her wrist, with the gem-stones that were also little buttons that you could press, and a place for her voice to go in, and one for the Guardian's to come out. But he was unable to understand how the words could travel between the two of them, and Olwen didn't have the right words to explain it to him. She was still trying when another floater appeared above them as silent as a moth, hovered for an instant and settled quietly on the turf below the grove.

"Why does he shine so?" Jody whispered, as the tall figure walked slowly towards them.

"He is made of an alloy, that is, a mixture of different metals, that is enormously strong and corrosion resistant. He doesn't frighten you, does he?"

"No, not really. He is very beautiful. It is just that when we speak of the Guardian of Isis, the Shining One, we mean something different from your friend, who is also a machine. It is very muddling."

"Truth is more than just words. Words can be twisted and their meaning changed, so that if you believe those twisted words you are believing a lie. But that does not change the truth that was behind the words in the first place. Before we spoke I had thought that when the vent through which the river flows was once cleared, then all would be well with your people. But it is not so simple. We have to clear two things, not one. We must set the river right on its true course again, and set your people right on theirs. And these two things must be done in a natural way, as grass grows from the wind-blown seed, and not by any 'miracles'. To do this we will need all the knowledge and logic that you can give us, Guardian dear." She smiled up at him, as his great height shadowed them both.

Jody saw the brilliant blue eyes meet the crystal facets in a message of understanding and trust that made him feel suddenly like an intruder.

"Sit with us, Guardian, and give us the benefit of your brain."

The Shining One doubled his body neatly, if a little stiffly, onto the ground between her and Jody. "The superstitions cannot be destroyed in a day," he said. "That is obvious. They took years to build, and may take as many years to undo. It is very comfortable to believe in something that explains the inexplicable. As long as the mesa and the mountains are taboo, the people need not concern themselves with upper Isis, or fear what it can do to them."

"The first settlers had breathers and ultra-violet-opaque suits," Olwen objected. "They could go where they wanted."

"But they did not feel comfortable with them, especially when they found out that you were free, that you did not need them. The suits and breathers must have made them feel alien to Isis."

"Is it better to live a lie and be comfortable?"

"Of course not. But it is certainly easier."

Jody thought it was about time to interrupt a discussion that looked as if it might go on pointlessly for ever. "If I tell the Council that you say that the mountains are not taboo any more, and that the thing in the Sacred Cave is only a communicator, they won't believe me. So what am I to do?"

"You will have to be patient and wait. That is perhaps the hardest thing of all to do."

"Be patient!" Jody felt as if he would explode.

Olwen smiled, and put a consoling hand on his arm. "Guardian, what is the best way of clearing the blocked vent, and ridding the people of the immediate danger?"

"Damming the river will be a simple matter, since it is out of sight of the village. But clearing the vent is another matter. We will have to use explosives. It will be a dangerous job placing them, and Jody will have to do it, if the water is as deep as I fear it will be by now."

"They will never let me near the Wall." Jody's eyes were wide at the idea. "They would kill me first."

"Guardian, think of a way of getting the people out of the way, so they do not see what you are doing. It must seem natural, nothing that they can make more stories about..." Olwen suggested.

The Guardian sat very still. Jody had the odd feeling that he had gone away, inside his own head. Then his eyes flashed, and his smooth face managed to look very pleased with itself. "If you are fit enough now, boy. It will be dangerous. Are you willing?"

"They are my people. I will do whatever you tell me."

"Then listen carefully, for there is a great deal for you to remember, and, once we have begun, the timing is everything."

121

Chapter Eleven

Jody returned to the Valley in a very different way from the way he had left it; and the journey, instead of taking more days than he had been able to count, took so little time that he could not even see that Ra had moved across the sky. The Guardian took him in a floater, skimming along valleys and up over the high cols between sharp-peaked mountains, following, like a clue, the fine thread of the river, his river, as it twisted its way south.

At first the Guardian kept the floater low, perhaps twice the height of a man above the ground, so that Jody was able to enjoy the sensations of flying without the paralysing fear of heights that had attacked him earlier. As they neared Cascade Valley the Guardian found it necessary to take the floater higher, and Jody was given an air-breather. By this time he was almost accustomed to this giddy mode of travel, and as he felt the cold, thin air of upper Isis against his skin he felt awake and alive as never before. He would have liked to shout and sing, but he hadn't the breath to do either.

"I wish we had floaters!" Jody exclaimed enthusiastically. "It would make light weight of our work."

"You had them once," the Guardian reminded him. "I surmise that your President had them destroyed or hidden. He did not want to risk any of you leaving the valley and finding me or Olwen. It is possible too that something twisted inside his mind to make him think that all science and invention is bad, because of what I did to Olwen. Perhaps the terrible conditions they left behind on earth made them hate technology—Mark London more than the others since he was the eldest of the children. But it is difficult to say precisely."

"It's not fair," said Jody hotly, understanding only a little of this. "He had no right to change all our lives just because he and the Lady Olwen..." He stopped, not knowing how to go on.

"What was between Olwen and Mark London is in the past. It is the damage of today that we must repair, and then slowly build a better way of living. But not by looking back."

Jody was silent, and the Guardian brought the floater down

low and allowed it to settle gently on the stony col above the Cascades. They had timed their arrival for the hour after dawn, and the eastern mountains cast a dark shadow across the Valley, although the sky overhead was filled with light and the mountains that rimmed the far west were pinked at their upmost peaks like spring buds.

Once the whispering hum of the floater was cut off there was silence, except for the background sound of the river that had been part of Jody's life from the beginning. It was like his own breathing and the sound of his own heart, and just because it was always there he never noticed it.

The Guardian touched his arm, and they left the floater and walked cautiously towards the knife-sharp edge over which the river poured. They crouched to look down the Valley. Jody looked down through the faint mist that he now knew was the atmosphere of the Valley, his eyes following the river into the lake and past the lake to where the river had once meandered through high marsh grass to the Place of the Wall. Now it was all under water. The river had spread to east and west, blotting out the casual loops of its meanders to form yet another lake that washed against the Place of the Wall.

Over to the west the first row of fruit trees was now ankle deep in water, and to the east the open area in front of the village was now no more than a narrow path. He was stunned to see how far the water had spread in the days it had taken him to find the Guardian.

"Not a moment too soon," the Guardian remarked calmly, and then added "NOW!" with such firmness that Jody was startled into scrambling to his feet before he remembered the plan and realised that the Guardian was speaking to Olwen through his communicator.

He dropped to his knees again, and his eyes followed the Guardian's pointed hand to the cliff-face of the mesa, still in the shadow of the eastern mountains. They watched as an indistinct figure appeared at the entrance of the Sacred Cave, a shadow among the shadows.

The figure lifted something . . . it was too far to see, but Jody knew that it must be the carved horn that hung at the cave entrance. A heart-beat later the sound came up to them, half-drowned in the constant noise of falling water.

A—hooo. A—hooo. A—hooo.

The last wailing note had barely faded away before the Village came alive. It was like seeing ants spill out of a kicked-over anthill. The ants ran this way and that in apparent confusion, suddenly to order themselves into a double line that curved northward to cross the river, high above the stepping stones, which must have long since ceased to be safe. Jody watched the tiny figures cross. One of them fell. An instant later the small sound of a cry floated up to them. The figure was helped up and the procession moved on.

The shadows of the mountains had not shortened noticeably by the time the whole line of people had been swallowed up in the shadow that was the entrance to the shelter cave at the foot of the mesa. The Guardian's crystalline eyes pierced the veil of mist.

"Could anybody be left?"

Jody shook his head. "No. Everyone goes, the old, the sick, the newborn. We would never leave anybody outside the shelter, once the warning horn has sounded the three-note."

"Is there any possibility of someone being outside the village, farther away?"

"So soon after dawn? No, Shining One, it is not our custom. Do not worry. Everyone on Isis is inside the cave. Everybody except you and me and the Lady Olwen."

He found himself grinning. It was an exciting idea, to have a whole planet to oneself like this. He wondered if that had been how the Lady Olwen had felt, back in the Beginning Times, when she was as young as he was, and the whole of Isis was her playground. It was no wonder that she had not wanted them to come.

He was startled by the Guardian's hand suddenly gripping his shoulder. "Quickly now. We have much work to do."

They ran back a short way from the edge of the Cascades to where the river followed a relatively flat course for a few paces, and where its banks were littered with scree. Together they began to dam the river, dropping loose flakes of rock into the water, man-handling larger stones and boulders.

At first it seemed that they were getting nowhere, and Jody began to wonder if the Shining One had not made some miscalculation, especially since he had insisted that the dam be built not straight across, but in the curve of a great bow, with the ends of the bow well beyond the banks of the river.

They laboured on without talking. Jody's healed hands cracked and his fingernails broke again. The thin air made him gasp. His chest hurt and he kept having to stop and use his breather. But he laboured on beside the Shining One, who worked without hesitation or effort.

Then the miracle happened. The river began to swell to fill the bow of stones. A trickle seeped through. Dried. They stood back and looked at it. Something happened to Jody's ears and he shook his head. Had he gone deaf? Then he realised that the voice of the river had stopped. No water flowed over the Cascades. Now there was indeed silence. It pressed on him, overwhelming.

"Stand aside!" The Guardian motioned to Jody, and drew from his belt an object that he recognised as a twin of one of the Gifts in the Sacred Cave, the one that had seemed to him to be like a weapon. The Guardian pointed it at the almost dry downstream side of the dam. There was a hum, and from the tool shot a thin straight line of brilliant red light. In spite of the warning Jody stepped forward to see what was happening, and the Guardian's free arm came up and smashed him to the ground.

He struggled to hands and knees, coughing painfully, the breath jolted out of his body. Then he scrambled awkwardly to his feet. The tool was now back in its place on the Guardian's belt. Where rocks, scree, gravel and sand had been heaped in an awkward curve, there was now a shining belt of melted and fused rock, as smooth as the inside of the Cave. Not a single drop of water could escape, and already downstream the wetness was evaporating into the thin air from the pebbles of the drying riverbed.

Jody coughed again and gaped. "What *was* that thing?"

"Never, never disobey me again!" The Guardian's voice was as even as ever, but his eyes flashed dangerously. "That laser beam would have made a hole right through your hand."

Jody dropped to his knees. "Forgive me, Shining One."

"Do not kneel to me, Jody. You know what I am."

Jody scrambled to his feet, feeling awkward and ashamed, and the Guardian put a hand lightly on his shoulder. "Come. Back to the floater. We have hardly begun our work."

So, for the first time in countless years, a floater entered Cascade Valley. It skimmed down river, past the place where the strange adventure had begun, where Jody had built his miniature water-wheel—underwater now. It had been a poor thing at best, thought Jody, remembering the wonders he had seen in the home of the Lady Olwen, and he sighed, discouraged.

"What is the matter?" asked the Guardian, as if what happened to Jody was of real concern to him.

Bashfully Jody told him about his invention, and the other inventions that had gone before. "But they don't *do* anything, and in any case nobody is a bit interested!" he concluded.

"You work and ask questions because *you* need to find the answers," the Guardian answered. "So why should you be concerned about what other people think of you? As to failure, do you not understand that every mistake and wrong turning on the way to a new discovery is in itself part of the discovery? Your people have been left alone to develop in your own way, not only by Olwen and myself, but also guarded from interference from passing space traffic by the message that the Light sends out. You must not be afraid to try, and when you fail you must ask yourself why you failed, and so on, step by step to a new knowledge."

"I really don't see why we were left to ourselves, if it is true that we came from a world clever enough to send us out into space. Why didn't they go on helping us, instead of abandoning us here?"

"If they had left you with everything that Earth had learned, then Isis would soon become a copy of Earth. You would have followed the same path and come much more quickly to the same dead end. Do you not understand that there are at every moment in your life a thousand choices, a thousand paths from which you may choose, if your minds are free to make that choice? Ahead of you is a network of possible ways to a future Isis, some very good, some as full of disaster as Earth's. But the route you choose must be *your* route."

"There is the computer in the Sacred Cave. Will you help me make that work again?"

The Guardian shook his head. "Now it would be a mistake. You have travelled too far down another path, and the

126

knowledge stored in the computer is irrelevant to your life. Don't regret it, or seek after what is locked inside the computer. It may well turn out in the end that the way you go is far better."

"President London's way?"

"No! His is based on lies and deceptions. It is a dead end. But if you put aside all the taboos and restrictions, you have a good life, do you not?"

Jody thought about it. "Yes..."

The Guardian sensed the reluctance in his voice. "But...?"

"It would be so much easier if we had floaters to get around in, and if we knew your way of storing air we could explore other valleys, and with lasers we could make our homes in the rocks too."

The Guardian smiled slightly. "Well, then, you must invent them, if you really need them. They must come *your* way, arising out of *your* needs, not put upon you from above. I think that in a way your people were wise to treat my gifts as things to have rather than things to use."

"But now I understand, you could help us so much."

"There will be no more gifts, Jody. From now on your people will be on their own. Once we have found a way to clear the passage for the river."

As he spoke he dropped the floater down to the shore of the lake below the village. "Test for me how deep it is, Jody."

Jody leapt from the floater and waded into the water until his feet touched the old shore line and he could feel the slimy grass under his feet turn to gravel. "It must be as high as the red mark on your measuring stick." He looked down at the thigh-high water.

"Beyond it, I'm afraid. You may come back now."

Jody floundered to shore. "Does it make much difference? Suppose we had got to it sooner?"

"We could have remedied the situation without danger. Now, I am afraid, we must use our second plan. I know you understand the dangers, Jody. I explained them to you. I would go myself, but although I am impervious to ultra-violet, cosmic radiation, even lesser dust storms, I have no defence against muddy water." He sounded almost apologetic. "You see, Isis is basically a dry planet, and I was never designed to cope with mud."

"It's all right, Guardian. I do understand. I will do whatever must be done." Jody spoke cheerfully. Their strategy had been thoroughly discussed and he understood just what he had to do.

But it was still only words. It wasn't until the Guardian had manoeuvred the floater so that it hovered above the centre of the new lake that lay within the Wall, that he began to realise exactly what was expected of him.

The Place, taboo to the people since his grandfather was a small boy, had a profoundly disturbing effect on him. There was nothing special to see. Just a circle of white stone-stuff surrounding a pool of oily-looking water. Perhaps that was it: the look of the water. It lay motionless, without the slightest ripple. It was like dead water, not living, and it was as dark as night, so that he could not see how deep it was anywhere. It could be only waist-deep. Or it could be a bottomless pit. He shivered, and hoped that the Guardian had not seen his fear.

"Put on the shoulder-harness first." The Guardian's voice was consolingly matter-of-fact. "The oxygen bottle goes here, in front, against your chest, so that you can get rid of it easily if you should get stuck. Now, the breather. The way I showed you, right inside the mouth. That is it. How does it feel?"

Jody spat out the mouthpiece so that he could talk. "All right, I suppose. But why can't I use the other kind of breather? This one makes me feel that I'm going to choke."

"You won't, I promise. And the other kind will not work under water, nor would it keep the water out of your mouth and nose and lungs. Trust me. This one will work properly."

Jody nodded, struggling to fasten the strange inventions to his body. "It's not ... it's just the idea of breathing under water. But I do trust you." He hoped his voice didn't sound as quavery as it felt.

"You must." The voice was stern. "You must believe in the breather and then forget about it, so that you can concentrate on what you have to do. Now the eye and nose piece goes on. Once it is in position you can breathe only through your mouth. Do you understand?"

Jody nodded. The Guardian fastened a cord of smooth slippery stuff, very different from the grass rope of the people, around his waist. The other end was fixed to the floater and lay in a neat coil on the floor. "Now we are ready. Don't use the mouthpiece until I tell you. I will position the floater exactly above the place where the river's exit vent should be."

"How can you tell?" Jody stared at the inky water.

"I have a map of all the vents and sink holes, and my eyes are not like yours. They see farther and in different ways. When I reach the spot I will drop a line with a weight on it. Then you must climb out carefully and feel your way down the line until you find the passageway through which the river should flow."

"I remember all that." Only now it was different, Jody thought.

"Kick your way down the passage as far as you possibly can. Only not too far. You must not let yourself become stuck. It should not be too bad. The water will help you and the sides will be slippery with mud ... not like that other time, when your grandfather became trapped. Once you have gone as far as you can, push the explosive ahead of you and let it go. Its own weight will help it to sink the rest of the way. Then you must get out."

The Guardian's voice as he repeated the instructions was as calm and emotionless as if he were telling Jody how to prepare a skin for the tanners. Yet he knew the dangers even better than Jody. When they had discussed the plan together back in Bamboo Valley the Lady Olwen had cried out, "Guardian, you cannot ask him to do that!"

He could hear her clear voice now, and remember her shudder, as she had whispered to herself. "It is my worst nightmare become real."

Now it was *his* nightmare. Could he really do it? Could he dive down into darkness, putting all his trust into the hands of this strange being, whom he had once thought was a god, but was really only a machine? Suppose he did get stuck, as Grandfather had done? The Lady Olwen would not be able to rescue *him*, nor could the Guardian.

"I would go myself, you know," he had told Jody and the Lady Olwen. "But my frame is too large."

"And your system would be ruined by mud," the Lady Olwen had said, and had added softly. "I cannot risk losing you."

For an instant Jody had felt very much alone, as the two old friends had looked at each other. They were strange creatures, the one immensely tall, limned with silver-gold light, the other white-haired and green-skinned. Yet the blue eyes and the crystalline had held each other's gaze with the same silent affection that he had seen pass between his grandfather and grandmother.

"I am not afraid," he had said loudly, breaking the spell between them. But he had felt diminished and he needed to assert himself.

"I am not afraid," he said now, looking down into the black oily water. Only this time it was a lie.

"Be afraid," the Guardian told him. He slipped the loop of the container of explosives over Jody's right wrist. "Just a little bit afraid. Enough so that you will not take unnecessary chances. If anything should go wrong, let go of the explosives and tug the rope twice. I will do my best to pull you out. But I cannot allow myself to get wet. You *do* understand?"

"I understand." Jody swallowed and managed to make his voice amazingly casual. "If I can't get back you must set the explosives off anyway. It will make no difference to me by then." It was a kind of trick, not to think too far ahead, and to do and say what was right.

Guardian did not answer, but skimmed the floater across the surface of the water, so close to it that the shadow of the floater almost touched it. He moved this way and that, very slowly, until he was entirely satisfied. Then he let the heavy marker go. It slid quietly into the water. The line ran smoothly out. Then slackened. It was time.

Jody took a deep breath and looked round. Ra had risen high enough to show itself above the eastern mountains, sending splendid pillars of light tilting across the grass-filled valley. Since the voice of the river had been silenced, the only sound was the soft speech of the grass. Its blooms shivered silver and red as the wind touched it with a giant hand and moved silently on. Everything looked unusually clear, its colours brighter, its outlines sharper. He identified separately all the subtle scents with which the soft wind was perfumed: the tang of thorn-bushes, the dryness of the upland grass, the dusty smell of red-grass pollen, the heady scent of an early golden cactus flower—and, binding them all together into a bouquet, there was the icy tang of mountain air, the air of upper Isis.

130

I have been up there, Jody thought triumphantly. I have been there and come back alive to tell my story. I have spoken to the Shining One and he has been as my servant. I have faced That Old Woman, the Ugly One, and she is beautiful and she has told me that death is a friend. It is enough.

He adjusted his eyemask, settled the mouthpiece confidently between his teeth and took a breath. It worked perfectly. There was no reason for more delay. He twisted the loop of the explosives container securely round his wrist, and then climbed onto the edge of the floater. It rocked slightly. He waited until it settled, and then dropped quietly into the water. He felt the guide rope rigid between the fingers of his left hand, ducked beneath the murky water and began to kick his way down.

He found it difficult at first. The water kept trying to push his body back to the surface where it belonged. Only the weight of the container helped pull him down. He floundered and then found a trick of scissoring his legs that took him down more easily.

He peered through the thick glass of his goggles, but he might as well have been blindfolded for all the good it did him. His flailing around had stirred up the silt, and it lay like a blanket around and above him, cutting out what little light should be coming from above. He found it less terrifying to pretend that it was night, to shut his eyes and feel his way down. He let his fingers follow the smoothness of the rope until at last they fumbled against the weight, half buried in mud.

Then he had to let the rope go. It was like letting go the hand of a friend. He waited, for what seemed a very long time, struggling with himself, before he was able to let his fingers release the rope. He felt downwards, past the weight. His fingers met slime, and beyond it rock. He stretched his arm downward in front of his face. More rock.

He kicked downward, committed now to this horrible dark tunnel. How wide was it? How far would he have to go? He stretched out his arms sideways and felt water-smoothed rock on either side. He could just touch the sides of the vent with his elbows if he flexed his arms.

Should he let the container go now? Its weight dragged his right wrist down. A twist of his hand and it would be gone. It would all be over. He could get back to the light. Why go on?

131

But the same drive that had forced him up over the Cascades and on the many days' trudge to Bamboo Valley would not let him take the easy way out now. Even while his brain was telling his hand to let the explosives go, his legs kicked strongly, driving him farther down the vent. He kicked again. A sudden grating noise, horribly magnified by the water and the enclosed space, shocked him into stillness. What was *that*?

His hands moved cautiously in the darkness ahead of him. They touched rock immediately. The vent must suddenly narrow here. It was the bottle of air on his chest, grinding against the rock, that had made that noise. He could feel the pressure now, painful against his breast-bone. Beyond this spot it was not possible to go. He had done what he must, and now he was free to leave.

He made himself take plenty of time to feel the limits of the space below him, so that he could drop the container precisely down the middle of the vent, with no chance of it snagging on the way down. He let it slip from his wrist, and it moved noiselessly down, out of his life, vanished as if it had never been. At once his body felt the urgent need to rise to the surface.

"Be very careful," the Guardian had warned him. "Use your hands to help you come out of the vent feet first. Do not attempt to turn, even though your body urges you to. If you should try to turn round in that narrow aperture you will be jammed in the vent and there will be nothing I can do to help you."

Even as the words echoed in Jody's head he could feel his body turning, wanting to rise to the surface of the water like a fish feeding in the dusk. He put his hands against the walls of the vent, forcing his body to remain as straight and stiff as a cane of bamboo. Slowly he eased his way backward.

It was a struggle all the way. Even while his body strove to bob up to the top of the water like a fishing float, its shape was all wrong to get there backwards. The water forced itself against the inside of his thighs, against his armpits, his chin. He floundered and struggled backwards and up. The walls fell away to left and right until he could no longer touch them both at the same time. He began to feel mud and slime instead of hard rock, and at last recklessly twisted his body around so that he was right way up again, and with a mighty push of arms and legs drove the water back.

132

He shot from inky darkness into the full light of Ra, which was lying on the surface of the water like white fire. He broke through and the light shattered into a thousand dancing pieces of silver. He spat the mouthpiece out and took a great gulp of real air. It tasted wonderful.

His eyepiece ran with water and he shook his head to clear it. He felt the Guardian's metal hands grasp his wrists and lift him back into the floater, where he lay dripping water and mud until his breath came back. Then he pulled off his eyepiece and sat up. He looked slowly round. Ra filled the valley with its clear pale light. He had never seen anything as beautiful as that light.

He let out a yell of pure joy. He couldn't help himself. It was just as if he had been reborn. But this time was different. The first time he had had no say in the matter. He had come onto Isis as a member of the N'Kumo family, the youngest of the Thirds, an afterthought.

This second birth was the birth of Jody N'Kumo, man. Himself. So he yelled, a yodel of uncontainable joy that echoed back to him from the mesa and the mountains.

The Guardian seemed to be neither surprised nor shocked. He lifted the floater from the surface of the water until it hovered steadily at arm's length above it. Then he leaned over the side, pointing a small metal box downwards at the water, which still rippled and threw back the broken light of Ra from the exuberance of Jody's rebirth.

"What is that thing?"

"It is a radio device. It has started the detonating mechanism. We have five minutes."

Jody had time to wonder how long "five minutes" was, as the Guardian sent the floater gliding along the dry river bed, and then up, up the jagged steps that until today had been forever veiled by the tumbling waters of the Cascades.

He parked the floater on the short turf and stones at the top. "Now we shall see!" He strode, gigantic and golden, to the edge of the cliff that had been the top of the waterfall. Jody wondered what they were waiting for. The Guardian and the Lady Olwen had explained to him that an explosive, properly placed, should be able to force open the blocked vent and allow the river to flow along its former passage. Only what was an explosive?

He had not long to wait. He felt it first as a tremor through the

133

soles of his feet, like that other thing that had shaken the Valley just before Thanksgiving. Then the still water within the Wall heaved, as if a giant were turning over. A spout of blackness shot into the air and fell back foaming onto itself. The stillness of the lake was shaken with splashing rock and scummed over with foam.

Then came the sound. It was a deep complaining roar from within the earth that mixed itself up with the noise of splashing water. Then there was silence. The lake grew still and there was only the foam to show that anything had happened at all.

Jody watched, puzzled. Had it worked, this explosive thing? Then, as he watched, it seemed that the Wall about the Place was growing taller, pushing itself out of the lake towards the sky the way a weed grows. The wind and sun brought tears to his staring eyes and he blinked and rubbed them. It was true. Through the faint valley mists he could see that the Wall was growing. It was the most frightening magic of all, and he cried out and covered his eyes.

"Watch!" said the Guardian and pulled his hands away.

The Wall grew taller still, and mud appeared at its feet. At last Jody understood. It was not that the Wall had grown, but that the water was rushing away, fast, down a great hole in the centre of the Place. Even while he watched a swirling appeared on the surface of the water, and in its centre grew a hole. Round and round the water spun, until the hole had sucked up the last of it. The lake within the wall was gone, leaving only a muddy swamp and a few puddles that reflected the blue-green sky. Even as he watched, the heat of Ra snatched at the wetness, and tendrils of mist smoked up and drifted away on the mountain wind.

"It worked!" Jody yelled triumphantly. "Your explosive did it!"

"We did it together, Jody. But now comes the final test—to release the river again, and see if the passage is totally clear. Stay behind me while I work, and this time—obey!" He took from his belt the thing he called a laser and pointed it at the dry downstream curve of the dam that they had built so painfully in the dawn light. So much had happened.

The laser hummed. A thin thread of ruby light shot from it towards the centre of the dam. Straight as the weft thread from a shuttle it shot. Jody saw the rock begin to sag and melt, as if it were rock-bunny fat. A stone fell forward. Water gushed. There was a hissing, and a cloud of steam rose as the pent-up water on the upstream side of the dam forced itself against the hot yielding rock. At last, with a roar, it was through, pushing aside the remains of the dam, racing to the cliff edge, smoking downwards to hit the valley floor. Spray hung in the air and Ra's bow formed itself again above the Cascades.

The Guardian pointed south. They saw the silver thread reach the lake and reappear at its southern end, to wriggle lazily through the marsh grass until it vanished into the archway in the Wall. Beyond the Wall they could just see its glint as it moved through the marsh grass as if seeking its accustomed path. It found it at last and vanished.

From behind Jody the river poured down from the high country. Cold, as clear as the crystals of the Guardian's eyes, life-bringing, necessary, it surged through the Valley and vanished, to reappear, Jody remembered, among other mountains, to nourish other valleys.

"A very satisfactory conclusion." The Guardian's clipped voice broke into his thoughts. "Without you it could not have been done. Thank you, Jody."

Jody blushed. "That's all right. I'm glad it was me. I mean ... it was..." He stopped. How could he describe the feeling of being reborn? But to the Guardian he did not have to. The metal head nodded and the crystalline eyes flashed Ra's light.

"I understand. I compute you as fulfilled. Grown. It is good. I must leave you now, Jody. I must check the springs in the southern valley to make sure that the whole course of the river is clear."

"Let me come too."

"I must go high. Does not the idea of floater travel fill you with fear?"

Jody thought back to the horror of the mud-filled vent. Of being suspended upside down in the blackness of the murky sludge. He laughed out loud.

The Guardian looked at him, his face impassive. "Humans are strange. I see that the greater fear has chased away the lesser. Yet nothing has actually changed..."

"Except me."

"Yes. That is so. You may come. We will get the floater clear

135

of your Valley, and then notify Olwen that all is well. Your people have had a long and anxious wait in the storm cave, wondering what damage the 'earthquake' has caused."

Jody felt a twinge of guilt. In all the excitement he hadn't given a single thought to his family, nor any of the others. They might have treated him badly, but they were his people and he should have remembered.

"Come, then. Climb aboard!"

The Guardian skimmed the floater south across the Valley, and then up and over the col between two of the great mountains that rimmed Cascade Valley. They followed a twisting course that avoided the highest mountain peaks. Almost immediately Jody lost all sense of direction. All he could tell was that Ra still lay, after each twist and turn, over his left shoulder; but which way they travelled or how far he never knew.

At last, as effortlessly as a stone skipped across the lake, the floater skimmed one more of many cols between tumbling raw-rocked mountains, and descended gently into a valley on the far side. Jody looked about him eagerly, and then with a sense of disappointment. This place was very different from the broad grassy vale where he had spent his life, and different too from the colour and magic of the Lady Olwen's Bamboo Valley. It was more like some of the valleys that he had struggled along on his way north. It was long and twisting, with high mountains on either side that pushed their stoney flanks towards each other, so that the valley was pushed first to east and then to west, and at times almost vanished, becoming nothing but a narrow gorge.

But it was different. The predominant colour was brown and the reddish-purple of the rock. There was only a little silver grey of thorn bushes and upland cactus to bring relief. It was a silent valley too. There were no birds, no deer grazing on grass now dry and brown, no rock-bunnies, no mice pushing their curious noses out of their burrows. Even the high-sailing eagles were gone. The wind moaned down from behind them, rattling the dry thorn bushes and shivering the dead grass.

What was wrong? Jody looked around and realised that there was no water. The tumble of stones at the bottom of the valley had once been a river. The brown grass had once been blue. The smooth dry rocks had once been covered with the silver strands of waterfalls rushing down to meet and join other strands, to twist together, to become a living river.

"There!" The Guardian pointed to the slope of one of the mountains that formed the barrier to the north. Jody followed his shining arm. Was he seeing things? Was that a dark stain, like blood, on the red rock? A stain that became a trickle. Not only in one place but in ten. Water was springing from cracks in the rock everywhere, trickling, twisting, spreading out and joining together. It collected itself and poured down the rocky tumble of its old bed, touching the brown dead grass as it passed.

There was noise in the air now, of the many sounds of water against rock. The air began to smell sweet and fresh again. Jody clapped his hands. "We did it!"

"Indeed we did." The Guardian seemed gravely pleased. He talked softly into his communicator, and then turned back to Jody. "I will return you to your Valley and then go home to Olwen. She has been alone for long enough."

"You love her, don't you?"

The crystal eyes reflected Ra's fire. For an instant Jody thought the Guardian was going to challenge him. After all, it *was* a pretty stupid thing to say to a machine. Then . . .

"Love? She is my meaning." He said nothing more then, but gestured to the floater, and when Jody had fastened himself in, he handed him a breather. "Wear it all the time. I cannot return you the way we came. I must sweep around the eastern mountains."

"Why?"

"Your people are no longer in the cave. The 'alarm' is over now, remember. They must not see me or the floater."

"I still don't understand why. If you told everyone about yourself and the Lady Olwen, and about where you live and about how you saved the Valley, then all the stories of the President would be proved to be lies."

"And what will happen then, do you suppose?"

"He will be deposed. Nobody would believe him in anything any more."

"What would they do with him? Where would he go to get away from the shame of it?"

"Why . . ." Jody stopped. He imagined what it would be like to be as proud a man as President London, made little in front of all the people. There would be no way for life to be tolerable

137

for him. "But he was wrong, all the same," he muttered.

"Of course he was wrong. His spirit was wounded and he was filled with guilt. He insulted my Olwen, but she bore *her* sorrow alone, not hurting him or any of you. You must do the same."

Jody sighed as he hooked the air-breather onto his face. "The Lady Olwen is wise and good. I'm not a bit like that."

The Guardian moved a switch and the floater hovered just above the parched ground. "Olwen was once a girl of your age, full of temper and impatience," he reminded Jody.

Since Jody could not talk comfortably through the breather he was forced to let the Guardian have the last word. The floater shot straight up until it was hovering eagle-high above the twisted valley. Already he could see how the fresh water was beginning to heal the hurt.

The floater rose higher still, until the tips of the mountains were beneath them, and his skin prickled against the cold air and the power of Ra's rays. He would not have believed that a human being could travel so high and still live; and he blessed his black skin that made a journey safe for him that might spell sickness or even death for his paler friends.

Below him lay a rose-red wrinkled landscape as far as he could see. What he was seeing now was the true surface of Isis. It was a planet of mountains, with only a few low places where his kind could bring up their families in health and safety.

The Guardian did not remain at these dangerous altitudes for more than a few heartbeats, but skimmed the floater north, slowly sinking until they almost grazed the rose-red tips. Then there was a sudden turn to the west, a skim across a high col and Jody found himself on familiar ground again, the flat place just above the Cascades.

Jody climbed out almost regretfully and looked around him. At his feet the newly restored river ran crystal-clear, sliding in a glassy curve to the depths below. The sound of falling water pounded in his ears, as familiar to him as the sound of his own blood. He stepped close to the edge, so that he could see the whole of Ra's bow suspended on the spray that rose from the foamy pool far below. Beyond the churning water the river ran down to the lake, which lay so still that the fruit trees at its rim seemed to be growing upside down in the water. Lazily it looped across the marsh to the Wall and vanished beneath the archway.

Jody could look at the forbidden place without fear. The marsh grass had already dried and sprung erect again. Within a few days the sedge and grasses would regain their healthy blue-green colour. The river ran straight and true into its passage beneath the ground, as it was meant to do, as it had done for aeons past, as it would do for aeons in the future. Unless...

"Could it ever happen again, Guardian?"

"It is unlikely. But if it should happen you will know what to do. There is a laser among the Gifts in the Cave."

"I might not be here."

"There will be others you can teach. Mark London is an old man. He will not be President for ever. Not this time perhaps, but next, when you are ready, it will be your turn. There will be a time when the leadership will go, not to the man who shouts the loudest, but to him with the boldest clearest vision. Then you will know that it is your time."

"If they knew that I helped save them, then maybe..."

"No! That must remain between you and me and Olwen. If your people knew what we had done today we would become more like gods even than before, and as for you, you might become their priest, but you could never be their leader. Be patient, Jody. Grow and learn, and never forget to hold onto the truth. Your time *will* come. It took millions of years for the wind and the rain and the rivers to carve a valley for you on Isis. You can learn to be patient for just a little while longer. Now I must go back to Olwen. Goodbye."

Jody held out his hand. "Will I see you again?"

"I do not anticipate such a meeting."

"I hate to say goodbye for ever."

"I understand your feelings of regret. I myself experience a certain reluctance to leave."

"You *do* have feelings, then?"

"It is unlikely and irrelevant. Goodbye, Jody N'Kumo. In the time of your ancestors in East Africa you would now be honoured as a man, a lion-killer. There are no lions on Isis, but you have faced death and conquered fear. Goodbye, Lion-killer." The Guardian clasped Jody's hand in his own metallic one.

"Thank you. I wish that ... well, I'm not sure how I'm going to explain things to people when I get back." Jody frowned.

"I believe you will find the right words."

"I suppose I will. I have to, don't I?" Jody nodded. "Don't wait for me. I will go down the Valley soon, but I need to think for a little."

Guardian let go Jody's hand, almost reluctantly. The floater left as quietly as an eagle soaring, and after Jody had watched it dwindle to a dot, to an empty sky, he turned and looked down at the Valley below the Cascades.

It would soon be time for him to go home, but first he must work out what he was going to say. To do it, without making more lies...

A tremor beneath the ground had caused the river's path to be blocked. That was true, and should not be too difficult to suggest as an explanation. Then clearly, the tremor that the people would have felt and heard while they were in the shelter cave had cleared it. No need to say whose hand had caused the second tremor ... though it *was* a pity. For a second he thought about the glory that might be his, and then he shrugged and laughed.

His lower lip jutted out. It was time to go home, to go on being Jody N'Kumo, son of Isaac, grandson of Jody, the youngest of the Thirds. As such he would be accepted back, now that all was well with the Valley.

But he was also of the N'Kumo people, of East Africa on planet Earth. He would remember that he was also a Lion-killer. He would be quiet, but he would never forget. Then, one day, not too far into the future, he would lead his people out of their narrow Valley and show them the rest of their new world. Eagerly he began the difficult climb down the cliff beside the Cascades.